Gabi heard t ... **turned, assu** ... **staff to clear the remnants of ... wedding away.**

Instead it was Alim.

"I was just..." Gabi started.

Just what?

Thinking about you.

She was one burning blush as he walked across the room, and she did not know where to go or what to do with herself as he approached the old gramophone.

And then she shivered.

Not because it was cold, for the air was perfectly warm. Instead she shivered in silent delight as she heard the slight scratch of the needle hitting the vinyl. The sounds of old were given life again and etched forever on her heart now. He turned around and walked toward her and, without a word, offered her this dance.

And, without a word, she accepted.

"Listen." He spoke into her ear and his low voice offered a delicious warning. "I am trouble."

"I know that."

"If you like me, then doubly so."

"I know all of that," Gabi said.

The trouble was, right now, here in his arms, Gabi didn't care about trouble...so she lifted her face to his.

Billionaires & One-Night Heirs

Secret babies they are determined to claim!

Raul, Alim and Bastiano—three billionaires
renowned the world over for their charisma
and commanding ways.

Lydia, Gabi and Sophie—three innocents
who cannot resist their seductive appeal.

And when sizzling nights lead to nine-month
consequences, there is no other option—
these billionaires will claim their heirs!

The Innocent's Secret Baby

Bound by the Sultan's Baby

Available now

Sicilian's Baby of Shame

Coming soon!

You won't want to miss this addictive new trilogy
from *USA TODAY* bestselling author
Carol Marinelli!

Carol Marinelli

BOUND BY THE SULTAN'S BABY

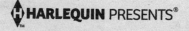

HARLEQUIN PRESENTS®

Recycling programs
for this product may
not exist in your area.

ISBN: 978-0-373-06063-4

Bound by the Sultan's Baby

First North American publication 2017

Copyright © 2017 by Carol Marinelli

Printed in U.S.A.

Carol Marinelli recently filled in a form asking for her job title. Thrilled to be able to put down her answer, she put "writer." Then it asked what Carol did for relaxation and she put down the truth—"writing." The third question asked for her hobbies. Well, not wanting to look obsessed, she crossed her fingers and answered "swimming"—but given that the chlorine in the pool does terrible things to her highlights, I'm sure you can guess the real answer!

Books by Carol Marinelli

Harlequin Presents

Billionaires & One-Night Heirs
The Innocent's Secret Baby

One Night With Consequences
The Sheikh's Baby Scandal

The Billionaire's Legacy
Di Sione's Innocent Conquest

Irresistible Russian Tycoons
The Price of His Redemption
The Cost of the Forbidden
Billionaire Without a Past
Return of the Untamed Billionaire

Harlequin Medical Romance

Their Secret Royal Baby

Paddington Children's Hospital
Their One Night Baby

The London Primary Hospital
Playboy on Her Christmas List

Visit the Author Profile page at Harlequin.com for more titles.

CHAPTER ONE

GABI DERAMO HAD never been a bridesmaid, let alone a bride.

However, weddings were her life and she thought about them during most of the minutes of her day.

From way back she had lived and breathed weddings.

Gabi was a dreamer.

As a little girl, her dolls would regularly be lined up in a bridal procession. Once, to her mother's fury, Gabi had poured two whole bags of sugar and one of flour over them to create a winter wedding effect.

'Essere nerre nuvole,' her mother, Carmel, had scolded, telling her that she lived in the clouds.

What Gabi didn't tell her was that at each wedding she made with her dolls, she pretended it was her mother. As if somehow she could conjure her father's presence and make it so that he had not left a pregnant Carmel to struggle alone.

And while Gabi had never been so much as kissed, as an assistant wedding planner she had played her part in many a romantic escape.

She dreamt of the same most nights.

And she dreamt of Alim.

Now Gabi sat, flicking through the to-do list on her tablet and curling her long black hair around her finger, trying to work out how on earth she could possibly organise, from scratch, an extremely rushed but very exclusive winter wedding in Rome.

Mona, the bride-to-be, stepped out of the changing area on her third attempt at trying on a gown not of Gabi's choice.

It didn't suit Mona in the least—the antique lace made her olive skin look sallow and the heavy fabric did nothing to accentuate her delicate frame.

'What do you think?' Mona asked Gabi as she turned around to look in the mirror and examined herself from behind.

Gabi knew from experience how to deal with a bride who stood in completely the wrong choice of gown. 'What do *you* think, Mona?'

'I don't know,' Mona sighed. 'I quite like it.'

'Then it isn't the gown for you,' Gabi said. 'Because you have to *love* it.'

Mona had resisted the boutique owner's guidance and had completely dismissed Gabi's suggestion for a bright, white, column gown with subtle embroidery. In fact, Mona hadn't even tried it on.

Gabi's suggestions were dismissed rather a lot.

She was curvy and dressed in the severe, shapeless dark suit that her boss, Bernadetta, insisted she wear, so brides-to-be tended to assume that Gabi had no clue where fashion was concerned.

Oh, but she did.

Not for herself, of course, but Gabi could pick out the right wedding gown for a bride at fifty paces.

And they needed this to be sorted today!

Bernadetta was on leave and so it had fallen to Gabi to sort.

It always did.

The bigger the budget, the trickier the brief, the more likely it was to have been put into the 'Too Hard' basket and left for Gabi to pick up.

They were in the lull between Christmas and New Year. The wedding boutique was, in fact, closed today, but Gabi had many contacts and had called in a favour from Rosa, the owner, who had opened up just for them.

Rosa would not push them out, but they had to meet Marianna, the functions co-ordinator, at the Grande Lucia at four.

'Why don't you try Gabi's suggestion?' Fleur, the mother of the groom, said.

It was a little odd.

Usually this trip would be taken with the mother of the bride or her sister or friends, but it would seem that it was Fleur who had first and last say in things.

Fleur was also English, which meant that, in order to be polite, Gabi and Mona did not speak in Italian.

Yes, it was proving to be a long, tiring day.

And they would be back tomorrow with the bridesmaids!

Reluctantly, *very* reluctantly, Mona agreed to try

on Gabi's suggestion and then disappeared with the dresser.

As Rosa hung up the failed gown she saw that Gabi was looking at another dress.

Silver-grey, it was elegant and simple and in a larger size, and when Gabi held it up she saw the luxurious fall of the fabric. Rosa was a talented seamstress indeed.

'It would fit you,' Rosa said.

'I doubt it.' Gabi sighed wistfully. 'It's beautiful, though.'

'The order was cancelled,' Rosa said. 'Why don't you go and try it on? It would look stunning, I am sure.'

'Not while I'm working.' Gabi shook her head. 'Anyway, even if it did fit, when would I get a chance to wear it?' Her question went unanswered as the curtains parted and a smiling Mona walked out.

'Oh, Mona!' Gabi breathed.

The dress was perfect.

It showed off Mona's slender figure, and the bright white was indeed the perfect shade against her olive skin.

'If only she had listened to you in the first place,' Fleur muttered. 'We are going to be late for the hotel.'

'It's all taken care of,' Gabi assured her, checking her list on her tablet. 'We're right on schedule.'

Ahead of it, in fact, because now that the dress had been chosen, everything else, Gabi knew, would fall more easily into place.

Measurements had already been taken but fitting

dates could not yet be made. Gabi assured Rosa she would call her just as soon as they had finalised the wedding date.

They climbed back into the car and were driven through the wet streets of Rome towards the Grande Lucia but, again, Mona wasn't happy. 'I went to a wedding at the Grande Lucia a few years ago and it was so...' Mona faltered for a moment as she struggled with a word to describe it. 'Tired-looking.'

'Not now it isn't.' Gabi shook her head. 'It's under new management, well, Alim has been...' It was Gabi who now faltered but she quickly recovered. 'Alim has been the owner for a couple of years and there have been considerable renovations; the hotel is looking magnificent.'

Even saying his name made her stumble a little and blush.

Gabi saw Alim only occasionally but she thought about him a lot.

Their paths rarely crossed but if Gabi was organising a wedding at the Grande Lucia and Alim happened to be in residence at the time then her heart would get a rare treat, and she was secretly hoping for one today.

'Let's just see how you feel once you've actually seen the Grande Lucia for yourself,' Gabi suggested. 'Remember, though, that it's terribly hard to get a booking there, especially at such short notice.'

'Fleur doesn't seem to think it will be a problem,' Mona said with a distinct edge to her voice, and Gabi watched as she shot a look towards the mother of the groom. From all Gabi had gleaned, Fleur had agreed to finance the wedding on the condition that it was held there.

'It won't be,' Fleur responded.

Gabi wasn't so sure.

Marianna, the co-ordinator, was rather inflexible at the best of times and they wanted this wedding to be held in just over two weeks!

They made good time as the streets were comparatively empty. The rush of Christmas was over and even the Colosseum was closed to visitors.

Gabi stifled a yawn, wishing that she could put up her own *Do not disturb* sign to the world for a while.

She had hoped to spend the Christmas break going over the plans for starting her own business. Instead, she had again been called in to work through her leave. She was tired.

Almost too tired to keep alive the dream of one day owning her own business.

She had started working for Matrimoni di Bernadetta when she was eighteen and had hoped that it would provide the experience she needed to one day go it alone.

Six years later, at the age of twenty-four, that prospect seemed no brighter.

Bernadetta had made very sure of that—there was barely time to think, let alone act on her own dreams.

Still, she truly loved her job.

Gabi looked up as the gorgeous old building came into view and they soon pulled up at the entrance.

The car door was opened for them by the door-man, Ronaldo.

'Ben tornato,' Ronaldo said, and Gabi realised that it was Fleur and not she he was welcoming back.

Fleur must be a guest. And a favoured one too from the attention that Ronaldo gave her.

As Gabi got out there was a flutter of excitement at the thought that she might soon see Alim.

He was always polite, even if he was somewhat aloof. She didn't take it personally. Alim was the same with everyone and maintained a certain distance. There was just an air of mystery to him that had Gabi entranced. An entire floor of the Grande Lucia served as Alim's residence when he was in Rome, and so, through the hotel industry grapevine, Gabi knew more than a little of his reputation. He loved beautiful women and dated as many of them as he could—though one night with him was all they would ever get.

Breakfast was definitely not included in this particular package. In fact, according to Sophie, a friend of Gabi's and a maid at the Grande Lucia, cold and callous were the most frequent words used to describe him by his lovers after they had been discarded.

That didn't seem right to Gabi for she always felt warm in his gaze, and when it came to business, his professionalism was never in doubt.

Still, Sophie had told her, for all the tears there were perks for, rumour had it the reward for time spent in Alim's arms came in the shape of a diamond.

It sounded crass.

Until you saw Alim.

He was completely out of her league, of course, and that was not her being self-effacing. He veered towards slender blondes of the supermodel kind, and women who definitely knew the ropes in the bedroom.

Apparently he had no inclination to teach.

Gabi didn't mind in the least that Alim was utterly unattainable, for it made it safe for her to dream of him.

There was no sign that he was there when she walked through the brass revolving doors and into the magnificent foyer of the Grande Lucia.

It was *almost* perfection.

Stunning crimson carpet and silk walls were elegant—even sensual, perhaps—and worked well against the dark wooden furnishings. The space was vast and the ceilings high, yet there was an intimate feel from the moment you walked in, alongside the lovely buzz of a busy hotel.

As a centrepiece, there was a huge, crimson floral display.

Yes, *almost* perfect.

Gabi had an eye for detail and this arrangement irked her. It never varied, or moved with the times. Instead, there was a perpetual display of deep red roses and carnations and it had become a slight bone of contention when Gabi had negotiated on behalf of her brides.

Marianna came to greet them and took the trio

for coffee at one of several intimate lounges just off the foyer.

There they went through a few details and though Marianna was delighted to announce that there was an opening in just over two weeks, she was not going to make it easy for the bride.

'I do need to verify dates with the owner,' Marianna said. 'We're expecting some VIP guests at the hotel in January so security will be particularly tight. I'm not sure we'll be able to accommodate you then. Alim has asked to be informed before any dates are locked in…' She paused and looked up. 'Oh, there he—'

Marianna halted, causing Gabi to glance up. Alim had just entered the foyer with the requisite stunning blonde.

Gabi guessed, and rightly so, that Alim did not like to be disturbed with minor details every time he made an appearance so Marianna did not alert Mona and Fleur to his presence.

Yet such was his charisma, both women looked over.

And while Marianna might be doing her best not to disrupt Alim's day, Gabi's had just been turned on its head.

In the nicest of ways.

He wore a slim dark coat and there was such an air of magnificence about him that he simply turned heads.

Not just for his dark looks—there was more to him than that—but they were rather wonderful to dwell on. His hair was black and glossy and swept back. He stood tall and his posture was so upright he always made Gabi want to pull back her own shoulders.

There was a shift that ran through her body whenever he was near, an awareness that made it difficult to focus on anything other than him, for all else seemed to move to the periphery of her consciousness to allow Alim centre stage.

'Quanti ospiti?'

Marianna's voice was coming from a distance and as she asked how many guests for the wedding, it was Mona who answered instead of Gabi.

For Alim had looked over and met her gaze.

He was beautiful.

Always.

Effortlessly elegant, supremely polite, he was the calm, still water to Gabi's fizz.

She was a dreamer, which meant that though he was out of her league, he was not out of bounds to her thoughts; innocent in body she may be, but not so in her mind.

And as for those eyes, they were a dark grey with silver flecks that spoke silently of the night.

His gaze was a dangerous thing to be held in, Gabi knew, and she was trapped in it now. There was a fire crackling in the grate and there was heat low, low in her stomach and rising to her neck.

She wanted to excuse herself from the conversation and walk over in response to his silent command. She wanted work to be gone, for his lover to disappear, and for Alim to lower her down onto a silken bed.

Just that.

'Gabi…' Marianna intruded.

'Alim,' his lover called.

But he was making his way over.

'Va tuto bene?'

He asked if everything was okay, and though his Italian was excellent, it was laced in his own rich accent and rendered Gabi incapable of response, for she had not expected him to come over.

It was Marianna who responded and told him the preferred date for the wedding.

'That would be fine.' Alim nodded to Marianna and to the other guests and then he looked directly at Gabi; she found herself staring at his mouth as he spoke, for it was just a little safer than to stare into his eyes. 'How are you, Gabi?'

'I am well.'

'That is good.'

He turned and walked away and she held her breath.

It was nothing—just an exchange so tiny that the others had not even noticed its significance, yet Gabi would survive on it for weeks.

He knew her name.

'Perhaps you could take Mona to see the ballroom while I discuss details with Fleur,' Marianna suggested.

Details being money.

'Of course.'

Gabi stood and smoothed her skirt.

Oh, she loathed the black suit with a gold logo and the heavy, cowl-necked cream top. It was the perfect outfit for a funeral director, not a wedding planner.

If it were her own business she would wear a willow-green check with a hint of pink. Gabi had already chosen the fabric.

And she would not wear the black high heels that Bernadetta insisted on, for she felt too tall and bulky as she walked through the foyer alongside the future bride.

And then she saw Alim and Ms Blonde stepping into his private elevator, and Gabi scowled at his departing back, for she envied the intimate experience they were about to share. Ms Blonde was coiling herself around him and whispering into his ear.

Thank God for gated elevators.

They were excellent for regaining self-control, for they slammed shut on the couple and as the world came back from the peripheries Gabi recalled that there was a wedding to be arranged.

There were large double doors to the ballroom and Gabi opened them both so that Mona could get the full effect as she stepped in.

It truly was stunning.

Huge crystal chandeliers first drew the eye, but it was a feast in all directions.

'Molto bello...' Mona breathed, and it was a relief to slip back into speaking Italian. 'The ballroom is nothing like I remember it.'

'Alim, the owner, had it completely refurbished. The floor was sanded back, the chandeliers repaired. The Grande Lucia is once again *the* place for a wedding.'

'I know it is,' Mona admitted. 'It is actually where James and I met. I was here for my grandparents' anniversary. James was here, visiting...' Mona stopped herself from voicing whatever it was she had been about to say. 'I just don't like it that Fleur is calling all the shots just because her...' Mona clapped her lips together. Clearly she didn't want to say too much.

Gabi, curious by nature, wished that she would.

Fleur was being very elusive.

From the draft guest list, the groom's side seemed incredibly sparse. Just a best man from Scotland would be flying in and that was all. There was no mention of James's father.

Gabi wondered if Fleur was widowed.

But Gabi wasn't there to wonder and her mind turned, as it always did, into making this the very best of weddings.

'Imagine dancing under those lights at night,' Mona said.

'There is nothing more beautiful,' Gabi assured her, and then pointed up to a small gallery that ran the length of the westerly wall and imagined the select audience watching the proceedings in days long gone.

'The photographer can get some amazing overhead shots of the dance floor from up there. A photographer I… I mean Matrimoni di Bernadetta regularly uses does the most marvellous time-lapse shots from the gallery. They are stunning.'

She could see that Mona was starting to get excited.

'When you say you were here for your grandparents' anniversary,' Gabi probed, because the thought of time-lapse photos had got her thinking…

'My grandparents were married here,' Mona told her. 'Sometimes they take out the record they danced to on their wedding night.'

'Really?'

'I even recognise the floor from their wedding photos. It's like stepping back in time.'

Yes, even the ballroom floor was stunning—a parquet of mahogany, oak and redwood, all highly polished to reveal a subtle floral mosaic.

'Your grandparents still dance to their wedding song…'

Mona nodded and Gabi could see that she was already sold on the venue.

There would be a string quartet, but Mona loved Gabi's suggestion that she and James dance their first dance to the same record that her grandparents had.

And a wedding, a very beautiful one, was finally starting to be born.

It was a rather more glowing bride-to-be who returned to the lounge area and now chatted happily with Fleur and Marianna about plans.

And it was a bemused Gabi who looked up and saw Ms Blonde angrily striding through the foyer;

she didn't know why, but she would bet her life's savings that Alim had uncoiled her, unwilling, from his arms.

Then later, much later, when plans were starting to be put more firmly in place, Gabi called Rosa with the official dates.

'I'm already working on the dress,' Rosa said. 'She's cutting it terribly fine to wear one of my gowns, even ready-to-wear.'

And, after a long, tiring day taking care of others, Gabi did something for herself.

She was all glowing and happy from that tiny exchange with Alim. Of course his lover's departure could have nothing to do with her, but Gabi was a dreamer, and already her mind was turning things around.

'Can I come and try on the silver dress?' she asked.

It was wonderful to dream of Alim.

CHAPTER TWO

IT TRULY WAS a beautiful wedding.

Not that Gabi had a second to enjoy it.

Resplendent in his kilt, the best man was being actively pursued by the matron of honour and doing his best to get away. Fleur was tense and asking that they hurry. The little flower girls were teary and cold as they stood in the snow for photos and Gabi felt like a bedraggled shepherdess as she juggled umbrellas for the bridal party and tried to herd the guests.

She was wearing boots, but that was the only concession to the cold.

Finally they were all in cars and heading off for the reception as Gabi ensured that the choir had been paid.

Bernadetta sat in her car, smoking, as Gabi shivered her way down the church steps.

And then it happened.

Gabi slipped on the ice and bumped down the last three stairs in the most ungainly fashion imaginable.

Not that anyone came over to help.

She sat for a moment, trying to catch her breath and assess the damage.

From the feel of things her bottom was bruised.

Pulling herself to a stand, Gabi saw that her skirt was filthy and sodden and, removing her jacket, she saw that it had split along the back seam.

To make things just a little bit more miserable than they already were, Bernadetta was furious, especially that Gabi had no change of clothes.

'Why haven't you got a spare suit with you?' she demanded. 'You're supposed to be a planner after all.'

Because you only give me two suits, Gabi wanted to answer, but she knew it wouldn't help. 'It's at the dry-cleaner's.'

And, of course, Bernadetta spitefully pointed out that no one else had one that would fit Gabi.

'Go home and get changed,' she hissed. 'Wear something…' And she took her hands and sort of exasperatedly pushed them together, as if Gabi was supposed to produce something that might contract her size.

And Bernadetta didn't add, as she always did to her other staff, *Don't outshine the bride.*

Gabi, it was assumed, hadn't a hope of that.

Oh, she wanted to resign, so very much.

Gabi was close to tears as she arrived back at her tiny flat and, of course, there was nothing in her wardrobe she could possibly wear.

Well, there was one thing.

The silver grey dress made by Rosa's magical

hands, though Bernadetta would consider her grossly overdressed.

Yet it was a very simple design…

Gabi undressed and saw that, yes, she indeed had a bruise on her bottom and on the left of her thigh.

In fact, she ached and was cold to the bone.

A quick shower warmed her up and Gabi was, by the time she stepped out of it, actually a lot more relaxed for the brief reprieve.

Wedding days were always so full on and it was actually nice to take a short break.

When she had her own business, Gabi decided, she would organise a rota so that all of her staff were able to take some time between the formal service and the reception. Perhaps there could be a change of outfit for them too…

Gabi halted.

She was back to hoping and dreaming that one day she might be working for herself.

How, though, when Bernadetta had her securely locked in?

Still there wasn't time to dwell on it now.

The dress had been a gift from Rosa but, feeling guilty simply accepting it, Gabi had splurged on the right bra to go with it and, of course, matching silver knickers, which she quickly put on before wriggling into the dress.

Rosa really was a magician with fabric—the dress was cut on the bias and fell beautifully over her curves.

And it deserved more effort than her usual lack.

Sitting at her small dressing table, Gabi twisted
her hair and piled it up on her head, rather than leaving it down. She put on some lip-gloss and mascara
and then worried that it might be too much because
usually she didn't bother with such things.

Yet she didn't wipe them off.

Instead, she dressed to look her best.

Tonight she didn't want to be the dowdy funeral
director version of Gabi, or the clumsy, fall-down-
the-stairs, eternally rushed wedding planner she appeared at times.

It was a split-second decision, a choice that she
made.

Gabi looked in the mirror. This was the person
she would be if she worked for herself and was or-
chestrating a high-class function tonight.

This was actually the closest she had ever looked
to the woman she was inside.

Gabi arrived back at the hotel, her stunning dress
hidden by a coat and wearing boots with her pretty
shoes held in a bag. Security was tight and Ronaldo, the doorman, even though he knew her well,
apologised but said that she had to show ID. 'There
are VIP's staying at the hotel,' he explained as he
stamped his feet against the cold.

'There often are,' Gabi said.

'Royalty,' Ronaldo grumbled, because royalty in
residence meant a whole lot of extra work!

'Who?'

'Gabi,' Ronaldo warned, for he was under strict
instruction, but then smiled as he chose to reveal—

it was just to Gabi after all! 'The Sultan of Sultans and his daughter.'

'Wow!'

Oh, she hoped for a glimpse of them—it sounded amazing!

Gabi handed over her coat at Reception and pursed her lips when she saw the large crimson floral display in the foyer.

The Grande Lucia was a wonderful hotel but it was like turning the *Titanic* to effect change at times.

Nervous, a little shy, and doing her best not to show it, Gabi returned to the wedding and walked straight into Bernadetta's spiteful reproach.

'If the bride had wanted a Christmas tree arrangement in the corner, I would have charged her for one,' Bernadetta hissed, and Gabi felt her tiny drop of confidence in her newfound self drain away.

'We need to check that the gramophone has been properly set up,' Bernadetta told her. 'And we need to find the key to the gallery for the photographer.'

'*We*' being Gabi.

She hit the ballroom floor running, or rather working away to make the night go as smoothly as possible for the happy couple.

Indeed, they looked happy.

Mona's dress was sublime and her groom was handsome and relaxed and...

Gabi frowned.

James reminded her of someone, but she could not place him.

Or was it just the fact that he was tall and blond,

like his mother, that made him stand out a touch more amongst the many Italian guests?

There was no time to dwell on it, though, and no time to acknowledge the ache of disappointment that Alim was nowhere to be seen.

And she admitted it to herself then, as she let the photographer up to the gallery and walked back through the foyer.

The dress, the pretty heels, the hair and the make-up…

In part they had been on the off chance that Alim might see her.

Alim was, in fact, in the building, but for once his presence was low key.

'I *hate* that we can't be at the wedding,' Yasmin moaned for the hundredth time, and pushed her dessert aside unfinished.

Alim said nothing in response.

He was very used to his sister's histrionics.

'We are shooed away like vermin,' Yasmin snarled, and threw down her napkin.

'Hardly vermin,' Alim drawled, refusing to be drawn in— they were sitting in the private area of the sumptuous restaurant at the Grande Lucia after all.

Their father did not join them for it would only draw attention, and that was everything Alim was doing his best to avoid.

At least for tonight.

The staff at the Grande Lucia were very used to esteemed guests but, Alim knew, they were starting to comprehend that Oman, the Sultan of Sultans, was in fact Alim's father.

Alim did not use his title in the workplace—Sultan Alim al-Lehan of Zethlehan.

Neither did he use it in his personal life, for it was a risqué personal life indeed. Diamonds paid for silence and there was the slick machine of the palace PR to wash indiscretions away.

Oman's main indiscretion was the reason they were here in the dining room tonight.

Close to the wedding but not present.

Tonight, when the happy couple headed to the bridal suite, Fleur, the groom's mother, would head to her own sumptuous suite of rooms.

Violetta, who dealt with palace PR and external arrangements, had taken over the arrangements of the guest rooms from Marianna.

Alim did not need to know, though of course he did, that Fleur's suite adjoined his father's.

Fleur was Oman's mistress of long standing.

She had borne the Sultan of Sultans his first son.

James had had a seemingly privileged life. He had been schooled at Windsor, had attended university in Scotland, and had a trust fund that would make most people's eyes water.

But his father's name did not appear on his birth certificate and he bore no title. To the people of Zethlehan he simply did not exist.

Yet he was Alim, Kaleb and Yasmin's half-brother, and they loved him so.

Kaleb, who was younger than Alim, would instead see the happy couple in Paris, where he currently lived.

The three of them together would turn heads indeed but subtlety was the aim on this night.

Yasmin, who lived a very sheltered life in Zethlehan, had pleaded to be a part of the proceedings.

Those fervent pleas from Yasmin had been declined by their father and so Alim had stepped in and offered to do what he could to enable Yasmin to observe the wedding from a distance.

Alim had arranged it so that he and Yasmin had been taking refreshments in the lounge when the bridal party had arrived back from the church, so that Yasmin could see the dress and everything.

Yasmin had enjoyed it immensely. 'What on earth is he wearing?' she asked about the best man.

'A kilt,' Alim explained. 'He's from Scotland.'

'Oh, it's so exciting,' Yasmin breathed.

A glimpse of the bridal party wasn't enough for her, though.

And though Alim had arranged that they eat the same meal and drink the same wines as the bridal party, it was a somewhat muted celebration.

The speeches would be wrapping up now, Alim explained, and he actually ached that he was not able to hear them.

'I want to see them dance.' Yasmin pouted.

She was very used to getting her own way.

But not in this, Alim promised.

There were volumes of intricate and ancient laws

and, until he himself ruled, Alim had no choice but to adhere to them.

Alim loved his country fiercely, and respected many of the traditions, yet from childhood he had seen the need for change.

For now, though, he tried to placate his young sister.

'You will see James and Mona tomorrow for breakfast; you can congratulate them then.'

'It's not the same, though!' Yasmin refused to be mollified. 'Why can't I slip into the ballroom for just a few moments and see them? You shall, Alim.'

'I shall only because I own the hotel and I often check in on functions. You would be noticed.'

Yasmin, like her brothers, had her share of the al-Lehan good looks and her entrance would be noted.

It would not take much for people to work things out.

Even so, Alim could not bear to see his sister unhappy—he knew how much Yasmin had been looking forward to such a rare occasion as a trip overseas.

'Listen,' Alim said. 'There is a viewing gallery in the ballroom.' He watched Yasmin's eyes widen. 'The photographer will be there now, setting up for photos, but after he comes down, you could watch things from there for a short while. I can give you a master key and you can go in a separate entrance from him and wait.'

'Yes!' Her eyes shone with excitement.

'Just for a little while,' Alim warned. 'The photographer will be back towards the end of the celebrations so keep an eye on him for when he leaves to come back up.'

'I shall.'

He gave her the key and further instructions and pretended not to notice that she swiped a bottle of champagne as they walked from the dining room.

Yasmin was very protected and afforded none of the freedom that Alim and Kaleb had been.

She deserved a little fun during her time in Rome, Alim thought.

So he led her to the stairwell and warned her *again* to stay low and to be quiet.

'Thank you, Alim!'

'Don't make trouble! Watch for a little while and then go to bed.'

Alone now, it was Alim who wanted to see his brother on this his wedding day.

And he also wanted to speak with Gabi.

Alim was a very astute businessman and he recognised Gabi's talent. He had worked very hard to bring the hotel up to standard but was aware that there was still much to be done. Marianna was very set in her ways and the more he thought about it, the more he wanted Gabi to be a part of his team.

Alim did not use the main entrance to the ballroom, for he wished to be discreet. Instead, he walked out through a courtyard and breathed in the cold air.

It was snowing and he stood for a moment listening to the applause as the speeches ended. The master of ceremonies was telling the guests that there had been another couple who had married here some sixty years ago and was leading into the first dance for the newlyweds.

Holding the wedding here and all that entailed had been the least he could do for his half-brother.

The staff might discover his royal status perhaps, but that was a small price to pay for being able to be somewhat involved in this day.

He wondered how his father felt, upstairs in the Royal Suite, as his eldest son married downstairs.

Alim walked in through the French windows and looked over at Fleur, who sat, a part of the bridal party yet somehow remote.

Alim held nothing against her—in fact, he felt for her. She had been a good mother to James and had never caused any problems for his family.

He, himself, was causing problems for a certain someone, though.

His entrance, however unobtrusive, could not have come at a worse time for Gabi.

Of all the moments that Alim could have chosen to check on proceedings, Gabi would have preferred that it was not this particular one.

Often he arrived with an entourage, but on this night he had slipped quietly into the ballroom just as the happy couple were about to take to the floor.

And *that* was the problem.

An old-fashioned gramophone had been set up and a microphone discreetly placed over it so that in this delicious old ballroom history would tonight be repeated.

Of course, there was a back-up recording to hand should the needle skid across the vinyl or start to jump, or should the assistant wedding planner's hand be shaking so much just at the sight of Alim.

He made her a quivering wreck simply by his presence.

He came in from the cold and, though impossible from this distance, she felt as if the cool air followed him in, for she shivered.

Do not look over, Gabi told herself. *Just ignore that he has come in.*

Under Bernadetta's less-than-reassuring glare, Gabi placed the needle on the vinyl and the sounds of yesteryear crackled into life. It was not the bride and groom who took to the dance floor—it was the bride's grandparents.

Tenderly, the elderly man held his wife and it was the perfect pastiche as the younger couple joined them.

It was an incredibly moving passing of the baton and just so utterly romantic to watch the elderly couple and the newlyweds dance side by side that it brought a tear to Gabi's eyes.

Oh, it made all the sleepless nights worth it, just for this.

She glanced up and saw that the photographer was snapping away.

They would be beautiful photos indeed.

Gabi went through her list on her tablet and saw that for now she was up to date.

Everything really had gone seamlessly.

'Another Matrimoni di Bernadetta success,' Bernadetta said, and Gabi's jaw gritted as her boss came and stood by her side. 'I hope that I can trust you to take it from here.'

Bernadetta made it sound as if she was bestowing a great favour when in truth she was skiving off early and leaving it all to Gabi.

All of it had been left to Gabi.

Bernadetta had flown back from her vacation just this morning and had spent most of the day staying warm in her luxurious car.

Gabi stood there, biting back tears as Bernadetta waltzed off, though of course she took time to network. Bernadetta knew very well which side her bread was buttered on, and was sweet and charming to anyone who might assist her ascent. She walked up to Alim, and Gabi saw her put her hands up in false modesty as she no doubt accepted congratulations from Alim for another hugely successful wedding.

And Gabi stood there, dreaming of one day going it alone.

Just dreaming of the day when she could call a night such as this *her* success and be the one Alim congratulated.

And that was how he saw her.

Lost in a dream.

Alim walked towards her and as she turned and looked towards him he smiled. She felt that she shone.

Criticism and fault were gone when she was held in his gaze.

No man had ever made her feel like that, no man had ever made her feel as if there was nothing, but nothing, that she needed to change.

He did that with just one look.

'I was wondering...' Alim said in that smoky voice of his, and so lost in her dream was Gabi that she put down the tablet she held and stepped towards him on instinct.

'I'd love to.'

And then she wished the ground would open up and swallow her.

Of course his arms were not waiting for her. Gabi had thought, stupidly thought, that he was asking her to dance, but instead, as he sidestepped, it was just a cringe-inducing faux pas.

Of all the embarrassing moments she had lived through, this was Gabi's worst.

'We're working, Gabi,' Alim said politely.

But no matter how skilfully he deflected or made light of her gaffe, not even he could save her from her shame as he told her the real reason that he had approached.

Of course he hadn't been about to ask her for this dance.

'I was wondering,' Alim repeated, 'if I might have a word.'

CHAPTER THREE

OH, THE SHAME!

Gabi wanted the dance floor to open up and swallow her whole.

Instead, she stood there as Alim gestured with his head, indicating that they move out from the ballroom.

When Alim asked to speak with someone, they tended to say yes, even if they would have preferred to run.

'The bride might need me.' Gabi floundered for an excuse. 'Bernadetta just left.'

'I know that.'

Alim had a word with one of the staff as they made their way out and told them where they could be found. 'If anyone is looking for you, you will be told.'

She retrieved her tablet and he led them out of the ballroom to a table and chairs, and as she took a seat he put up his hand to halt a waiter as he approached.

This was business.

Yet her navy eyes were shining with embarrassed

tears and there was a mottle to her chest from the mother of all burning blushes.

Poor thing, Alim thought.

He was terribly used to women liking him, even if it was a more sophisticated sandpit where he usually played.

Gabi would know that.

Surely?

'The wedding and the celebrations have gone very well,' Alim said.

'Matrimoni di Bernadetta put a lot of effort into it,' Gabi duly responded.

'I think we both know,' Alim said, 'that Bernadetta put precisely zero effort into this wedding.'

Gabi blinked at his forthrightness.

'Bernadetta isn't here,' Alim interrupted, 'so speak to me, Gabi.'

'Why?'

'Because I might be able to help. I appreciate hard work, I like to see talent rewarded.'

'I am well rewarded.'

He raised an eyebrow slightly.

The pay, they both knew, was terrible.

'I know that the gramophone was your idea,' Alim told her.

'How could you know that?'

'I know the groom. That is why I had to drop in and check that everything was going well.'

'Oh.'

'And he told me how impressed they were with you.'

Actually, the information hadn't been that forthcoming, James hadn't raced to tell Alim how wonderful the assistant wedding planner was.

Alim had specifically asked.

His success had come, not by accident, or by acquired wealth or by flouting his title. He kept his royal status as private as he could, and while his impossible wealth had been a starting point, it was his attention to detail that caused his ventures to thrive.

Alim did not merely accept findings, he dug deeper. And while he knew that Matrimoni di Bernadetta was amongst the top tier of wedding planners, he was very aware of the mechanics of the business.

Bernadetta had chosen well!

'Tell me.'

He could tell she was nervous.

'Why did you choose this career?' he asked.

'Because I love weddings.'

'Even now?' Alim asked. 'Even after…?' He asked a question. 'How old are you?'

'Twenty-four and, yes, I still love weddings. I always have, since I was a little girl.'

'And you've worked for Bernadetta for how long?'

'Six years,' Gabi said. 'Before that I worked for a local seamstress. And when I was at school…' She halted, not wanting to bore him.

'Go on.'

'I worked for a local florist. I used to work through Friday night to have the bouquets ready for weddings. I would get up to go to the markets before school…'

This was the passion Alim wanted in his staff.

'I was very lucky that Bernadetta took me on.'

'Why is that?' he asked.

'Well, I had no qualifications. My mother needed me to work so I left school at sixteen and Matromoni di Bernadetta has a good reputation.'

'So how did you get an interview?'

'I wrote to her,' Gabi admitted. 'Many times. After a year she finally agreed to give me an interview, though she warned me the competition was extremely tough. I had my friend Rosa make me a suit and I...' Gabi gave a tight shrug. 'I asked for a trial.'

'I see.'

'Bernadetta showed me a brief she had for a very important wedding and asked for my ideas.' Gabi gave him a smile. 'You've heard of fake it till you make it...'

'Fake what?' Alim asked.

'I pretended that I knew what I was doing.'

'But you *did* know what you were doing,' Alim said, and Gabi swallowed. 'You had already worked for a seamstress and a florist...'

'Yes, but...'

'And what happened with the ideas you gave her for this very important wedding?'

'She incorporated some of them.'

'So what part were you faking?'

Gabi frowned. 'I've learnt an awful lot working for Bernadetta.'

'Of course,' Alim agreed. 'She is at the top of her game. I have no hesitation recommending her. Still,

I know that lately most of the credit should fall to you. Have you ever thought about moving out on your own?'

Her blush had all but faded and now it returned, though not to her chest. He watched as her cheeks darkened and her jaw tightened and Gabi was angry indeed, Alim knew.

'I can't.'

'Why not?'

'Alim…' Gabi shook her head. She was loyal, even if it was misplaced, and she had also got into trouble for dreaming out loud before.

'Talk to me,' he said.

'Why?'

'Because I may be able to help.'

'Bernadetta found out that I one day hoped to go out on my own, and she reminded me of a clause in my contract.'

'Which is?'

'That I can't use any of the firms that she does for six months after leaving. I'd have to make new contacts.'

'But you already use only the best.'

'Yes.' Gabi nodded, glad that he immediately got it. She had spent hours trying to explain it to her mother, who'd said she should just be glad to have a job. It was so nice to discuss it with Alim! 'Those contacts weren't all Bernadetta's to start off with.' Gabi had held it in for so long that it was a relief to vent some of her frustration. 'The bride tonight is wearing Rosa's creation. It was her lounge floor that I used to cut fabric on.'

'Tell me,' he urged.

So Gabi did.

'When I first worked for Bernadetta we had a bride to dress and she had only one arm. So many of the designers shunned her, they did not want her wearing one of their creations. I was furious so I suggested that Bernadetta try Rosa. She scoffed at the idea at first but in the end agreed to give her a try—Rosa made the bride a princess on her day. It was a very high-profile wedding and so in came the orders. Now Rosa works in the best street in Rome. Rosa is *my* contact but of course I did not think to get that in writing at the time.'

Alim watched as Gabi slumped a little in her seat. Defeated.

And then he fought not to smile as her hand went to her hair and she coiled a strand around her finger.

For after a moment's pause she rose again.

Now she had started to air her grievances, Gabi found that she could not stop. 'The flowers today, the gardenias—it was the florist's idea to replicate the grandmother's bouquet.' Alim noted that Gabi did not take credit where it was not due and he liked that. 'The florist, Angela, is the woman I worked with when I was at school. We used to work in a tiny store, now she is known as one of the finest bridal florists in Rome.'

'So the best contacts are off limits,' Alim said, and Gabi nodded.

'For six months after I leave—and I doubt I could hold off for that long. That is assuming anyone will hire me as their wedding planner. I doubt Bernadetta will give a good reference.'

'She'll bad-mouth you.'

He said it as fact.

He was right.

Alim had thought he had the solution.

Right now, he could be wrapping the conversation up with the offer that Gabi come and work for him.

It was rather more complicated now, though, and not just because she liked him. Alim was very used to that.

It was that he liked her.

He acknowledged it then. Just a little, he assured himself.

But, yes, for two years the hotel had seemed warmer when Gabi was here. For two years he had smiled to himself as she clipped across the foyer in those awful heels, or muttered a swear word now and then under her breath.

He had never allowed himself to acknowledge her beauty but he could not deny it now.

She looked stunning.

Her hair was falling from its confines, her dress shimmered over her curves and how the hell had he not swept her into his arms to dance? Alim pondered. But the answer, though he denied it, was becoming clearer the longer they spoke—he had been resisting her for a long time.

The other week his mood had not been great.

Christmas was always busy in the hotel industry but it wasn't just that that had accounted for his dark mood.

Issues back home were becoming more pressing.

But it wasn't that either.

There had been a vague air of discontent that he could not place, though admittedly he had avoided seeking its source.

Alim had not wanted to give voice to it.

So he hadn't.

Outside work he had been his usual reprobate self, but some time between Christmas and New Year he had walked into the foyer of the Grande Lucia and seen that Fleur had taken him up on his suggestion that they use Matrimoni di Bernadetta to plan the wedding. They hadn't held a wedding here in a very long while and Alim had found that he missed Gabi's presence. The air felt different when she was around.

He fought to bring his thoughts back to work.

'What would you do differently from Bernadetta?'

Gabi frowned, for it felt like an interview, but she answered his question.

'I'd ditch the black suit.'

'You already have.' His eyes did not leave hers as he said it but he let her know that the change from her usual attire had been noted.

Oh, it had.

It no longer felt like an interview.

Their minds actually fought not to flirt—Gabi because she did not want to make a fool of herself again, and Alim because he kept work at work.

'There was a wardrobe malfunction back at the church,' Gabi carefully answered.

'Malfunction?'

'I fell,' Gabi said. 'Thankfully it was after the bridal party had left, but I tore my suit.'

'Did you hurt yourself?'

'A bit.'

He wanted to peel off her dress and examine her bruises; he wanted to bring her now to his lap.

But still his eyes never left hers and the conversation remained polite.

'So you would ditch the black suit in favour of what?

'I've seen this fabric, it's a willow-green and pink check, more a tartan. It sounds terrible but...'

'No,' Alim said. 'It sounds different. Do you have a picture?'

Of course she did, and she took only a moment to bring it up on her tablet and hand it to Alim.

He looked at the picture of the fabric she had chosen. It was more subtle than she had described and, yes, it would be the perfect choice.

'What would you change here at the Grande Lucia?' he asked as he handed back the tablet. He expected her to flounder, given that she'd had no time to prepare.

Gabi though knew exactly what the first change would be.

'There would be a blanket ban on red carnations throughout the hotel.'

She watched the slight twitch of his very beautiful

lips. Alim had many areas of expertise but flowers were not amongst them. 'I don't tend to get involved with the floral displays,' he said.

'I do.' Gabi smiled. 'I obsess about such things.'

'Really?'

'Really.'

'What would you choose?'

'Sahara roses are always nice, though I think it should vary through the week, and at weekends I would change the theme to tie in with the main function being held.'

'Would you, now?'

'You did ask.'

'Are Sahara roses your favourite flower?'

'No,' Gabi said.

'What is?'

'Sweet peas.' She gave him a smile. 'Marianna would faint at the idea and deny that they are sophisticated enough for the Grande Lucia, but, honestly, when arranged right...'

Her face lit up and he smiled.

Gabi was all fresh ideas and the zing of youth, and coupled with Marianna's wisdom...

But it was getting harder to think of business.

Very hard.

'Would you like a drink?' Alim offered.

'I'm working.'

And there was a slight ironic smile that dusted his lips as she mirrored his own words from earlier.

'Gabi...' Alim said, and then halted.

He needed to think this through before he offered

her this role; she had already been dragged over the coals. If she were to work for him, it could get messy. One-night stands were his usual fare and that was why he kept his personal life where it belonged.

In bed.

He wanted the best for his business and yet, rarely for Alim, he found that he wanted what was best for her, so he came up with an alternative.

'Have you thought of going into partnership with Bernadetta?'

'Partnership?' Gabi shot him an incredulous look. 'She would laugh me out of her office if I suggested it.'

'And when she had stopped laughing, you would tell her that you'd make a better partner than rival.'

It had never even crossed her mind.

'Or, if you continue to work for her you set your limits, you tell Bernadetta only what you are prepared to do. What works for you…'

He did not want to lose her though.

Oh, this could get messy, yet the closer he examined it, the more it appealed.

'There is another option…'

'Gabi!' Her name was said again and she turned as one of the waiters came over. 'The photographer wants to speak with you.'

'Excuse me,' Gabi said, and, ever the gentleman, Alim stood as she left.

Alim went back into the ballroom and looked up. He saw the westerly door open and smiled at the thought of Yasmin creeping in.

And then he turned and saw his brother.

There were no halves where love was concerned.

'Congratulations,' Alim said.

'Thank you.'

And that was all he could offer in public.

James's complexion and hair were lighter but standing side by side it would be hard to miss the similarities. They had to step apart before someone made the connection.

Alim took a call from Violetta and was told that the Sultan of Sultans would like to speak with him.

Things were already tense between Alim and Oman.

Oman resented Alim's freedom, and was bitter with his lot for Fleur was the love of his life. And, in turn, Alim, though respectful with words, was silently disapproving, for he loved his mother and loathed how she had been treated.

Alim bowed as he entered the Royal Suite and then told his father about the wedding's progress.

'Everything is going smoothly,' Alim informed him, though that knowledge did not make things better for Oman since he could not be there to see his son marry for himself.

'Where is Yasmin?' he snapped.

'We had dinner,' Alim calmly answered, 'and she is now in her suite. The reception will finish shortly; you will see James and Mona in the morning.'

No doubt, Alim thought, Fleur would be here soon.

He thought he would now be dismissed but, instead, Oman brought up an argument of old.

One that had never really left them.

'I want you home.'

Alim was in no mood for this but he did not show his irritation. 'I was in Zethlehan last month and I shall be back for a formal visit in—'

'I mean permanently.' Oman interrupted.

'That isn't going to happen.'

They had had this argument many times before.

Alim refused to act as caretaker to his country just so that his father could travel abroad more.

He would not facilitate the shaming of his mother.

Although he was happy for James and Mona and wished he could participate more in the celebration, tonight still felt like a betrayal to his mother.

'You are thirty-two years old, Alim. Surely it is time that you marry?'

Alim stayed silent but his eyes told his father that he did not need marriage guidance from a man who had a wife and a mistress. Alim never cheated. He was upfront in all his relationships, and there could be no confusion that what he offered was a temporary affair. Arrogant, some might say, but better that than leading someone on.

'I shall select a bride for you,' Oman said in threat. 'Then you shall have no choice but to marry.'

'We always have choices.'

The advice he had so recently given to Gabi had been tested over and over by Alim—he had long ago set his limits with his father and told him what he was and was not willing to do.

'To choose a bride without my agreement could

only serve to embarrass not just the bride but our country when the groom does not show,' Alim warned. 'I will not be pushed into marriage,'

'Alim, I am not well.'

'How unwell?' Alim asked, for he did not trust his father not to exaggerate for gain.

'I require treatment. I am going to have to stay out of the public eye for six months at least.'

Alim listened as his father went into detail about his health issues and Alim had to concede grudgingly that there was a battle ahead.

'I will step in,' Alim responded. 'You know that.'

It wasn't the response his father wanted, though, and he pressed his son further. 'Our people need good news, a wedding would be pleasing for them.'

Alim would not be manipulated and stood up to his father just as he always had. 'Our people would surely want to see the Sultan of Sultans at such a celebration. A son's wedding without his father's presence would send the message that the father did not approve of his son's choice of bride, and this could surely cause our people anxiety.' Alim watched his father's jaw grit. 'Let us discuss this again when you are well.'

His father would have argued further, but suddenly Alim sensed distraction as he saw Oman glance towards the adjoining door, and he guessed that his father's lover had just arrived.

'I shall see you in the morning for breakfast,' Alim said, and then bowed and left.

As he walked along the corridor, though outwardly calm, inside his mood was dark. No, he could not put off choosing a bride for ever, but he had no desire to live the life that his parents did—he thought of his mother alone tonight in the palace. Always she had put on a brave face and smiled at her children as if things were just fine.

How could they be?

Alim did not want a bride chosen for him by his father.

He wanted…

What?

The maudlin feeling would not shift. Alim reminded himself that his friend Bastiano would be in town next week and that would likely cheer him up. But Bastiano was just another rich playboy, and the casinos and clubs did not hold their usual allure for Alim.

In truth, he was tired of his exhausting private life. The thrill of the chase no longer existed, for after two years in Rome women sought *him* out.

He walked through the foyer and, sure enough, the last of the guests were leaving.

Alim went up the stairwell and, unlocking the door, he went onto the gallery.

There were no signs of his sister and Alim assumed she was safely in her suite. The photographer had left some equipment so Alim made a mental note to lock the door as he left.

Alim glanced down at the stunning ballroom.

The staff were clearing the glasses and tables away but most of it would wait for the morning.

It was done.

The wedding had been *his* gift to the couple and Fleur had engineered things so that it was held at the Grande Lucia. Yet he had not taken any significant part in the proceedings.

Yes, it had been a wonderful wedding but for Alim it had been a wretched day and night.

Apart from the time spent with Gabi.

He looked down at her standing in the now-empty ballroom.

Alim had been going to ask her to work for him but had decided that, given how he felt, at best it would be foolish to get overly involved.

Then he smiled when he recalled her blush when she had thought he was about to ask her to dance.

And, as of now, he was no longer working.

CHAPTER FOUR

GABI WANTED TO go home and hide her shame.

Over and over she replayed it in her head—that awful moment when she had thought the suave Alim had been asking her to dance.

She stood in the empty ballroom and surveyed the slight chaos that a successful wedding reception left in its wake.

The staff had been in and cleared the plates and glasses, the tables had been stripped and the chairs stacked away. All Gabi had to do tonight was take the old gramophone out to her car and safely put away the grandparents' vinyl record that the bride and groom had danced to.

It could wait a few moments, though, and Gabi paused to look around.

It was *such* a magnificent ballroom.

The chandeliers had been switched off and it was lit now by the harsh white downlights that had come on when the music had ended and it had been time for the guests to leave.

And, because she could, Gabi headed to the power

box and one by one flicked the switches until all the lights were off.

She did not turn on the chandeliers.

They didn't need electricity to be beautiful, for the moonlight came in through the high windows and it was as if the snow outside was now falling within. Even unseen trees made an appearance because the shadows of branches crept along the silver walls.

It was like standing in an icy forest, so much so that she could imagine her breath blowing white.

What had Alim been about to say to her?

It might be weeks or months before she was here at the Grande Lucia again.

Maybe she would never know.

Gabi heard the door open and turned, assuming it was one of the staff to clear the remnants of the wedding away.

Instead, it was Alim.

'I was just…'

Just what?

Thinking about you.

Gabi didn't say that, of course.

'It went very well tonight,' he said.

'Thank you.'

And now she should collect her things and go home, yet she made no move to leave.

She was one burning blush as he walked across the room, and she did not know where to go or what to do with herself as he approached the old gramophone.

And then she shivered.

Not because it was cold, for the air was perfectly warm; instead, she shivered in silent delight as she heard the slight scratch of the needle hitting the vinyl. The sounds of old were given life again and etched on her heart for ever as he turned around, walked towards her and, without a word, offered her a dance.

And, without a word, she accepted.

His embrace was tender but firm and, close up, the heady, musky sent of him held a peregrine note that she could not place. But, then, nothing about to-night was familiar.

Usually his greetings were polite; tonight things had changed and, Gabi thought, even the suave Alim seemed to accept they were on the edge of something.

'Listen.' He spoke into her ear and his low voice offered a delicious warning. 'I am trouble.'

'I know that.'

He felt her head nod against his chest and her words were accepting rather than resigned so he made things clearer. 'If you like me, then doubly so.'

'I know all of that,' Gabi said.

The trouble was, right now, here in his arms, Gabi didn't care and she lifted her face to his.

Tonight was her night.

Gabi knew his reputation and accepted it would never be anything more than a night, yet she had carried a torch for Alim for years.

The consequences she could live with.

It was regret she could do without.

His body she had craved and imagined for so long, and she rested against it now. He was lean and strong and he moved her so skilfully to the music that for the first time in her life Gabi felt not just co-ordinated but light.

They stared deep into each other's eyes. She never wanted to leave the warmth of his gaze, and for now she did not have to.

They stared and they swayed and they ached within.

His whole life, Alim had fought to keep his business and personal life separate. It had seemed the sensible thing to do, yet nothing made more sense than the thoughts that were now forming in his mind.

One woman.

He thought of the many upcoming trips home and he thought of returning to the Grande Lucia and to Gabi in his bed.

Alim thought of them working together and still it did not deter him, for there would be benefits for them both.

His head lowered, his lips brushed hers, and on contact Gabi knew she would never regret this.

A gentle kiss had been her fantasy, perhaps one on the cheek that changed midway.

Yet his kiss was decisive as his mouth met hers and he delivered her first kiss. She melted at the sheer bliss of it.

It actually felt as if her lips seemed to know what to do, for they moved and melded to the soft caress of Alim's.

He was used to slenderness yet his hands now ran over luscious curves; he felt the press of her breasts against his chest and suddenly there was less reason for caution than he had ever known.

He wanted Gabi in bed—and not just for this night—so he moved his mouth from hers.

'Are you seeing someone?' he asked.

And though she was held in his arms, though he was hard against her soft stomach, his question was so matter-of-fact and so direct that it felt again, to Gabi, like an interview.

'When does a wedding planner get time for a social life?' she murmured, keen to get back to his kiss.

'So it causes problems in your relationships?'

He was fishing, shamelessly so.

She was honest.

And not to her detriment.

'There have been no relationships.'

Her words went straight to his groin, and Gabi felt him further harden in response to them while his hands on her hips moved her further in.

As he met her mouth again, she felt the odd sensation of panic devoid of fear.

The intimate taste of him was briefly shocking, the intensity and the thoroughness of his kiss was better in the flesh than in dreams. There, in imaginings, she did not know quite what to do, but here, with him, she held his breath in her mouth and swallowed it as he accepted hers.

They made hunger.

Illicit.

That was the taste they made.

The tip of her tongue was surely nectar for he savoured it, and the scratch of his jaw was a new hurt for her to relish.

Her breasts ached against fabric as his hands roamed her curves, and she felt the dig of his fingers in her hips and the grind of him against her.

Dignity was not Gabi's forte.

She slipped and fell on so many occasions.

Tonight, though, she danced with the man of her dreams.

It was just a dance, she told herself. Her body denied it.

Oh, it was so much more than a dance.

He moved her an inch, a dangerous inch for it felt as if their heat met and she was scared to let go, scared to misread the situation again, but it felt as if they were headed for bed.

As she opened her eyes to the coolness of his cheek Gabi was ready for more.

It was the eyes of insatiable heat that met his.

'What the hell was I thinking?' Alim asked, for he still could not believe he had sidestepped that dance.

She did not understand the question, and since he offered no clarification Gabi did not attempt a reply.

Alim spoke for both of them.

'Come to bed.'

CHAPTER FIVE

HE TOOK HER hand and led her from the dance floor but as they reached the double doors he dropped it.

'For this to work,' he told her, 'we must be discreet.'

Alim was talking of the weeks and months ahead while Gabi was thinking just of this night, but nevertheless she nodded. Her cheeks were flushed and her mind was flurried with hormones like a snowglobe, and so she was grateful that he could think of sparing her blushes in the morning.

His thoughtfulness spurred her to think of tomorrow also.

'I need to get my coat, or they'll know that I stayed the night.'

'Do so, then,' Alim told her. 'Just say goodnight and that you are collecting some dresses...'

He knew her routines for he *had* noticed her... Often, before she went home, Gabi would head up to the dressing suite, where bridesmaids and such got changed, and leave the hotel with her arms filled with tulle.

She blinked at the fact that he knew.

'I'll head up,' Alim said. 'I have a private elevator...'

'I know that you do.'

'I shall send it back down.'

Alim left the ballroom and a moment later so too did she.

It was like any other night.

He walked to his elevator and pulled open the antique gate as Gabi smiled at Silvia, the receptionist on duty tonight.

'I just have to get some dresses and then I'm done,' Gabi said. 'Can I just get my coat?'

'Sure.'

Gabi slipped behind the desk and into the small staff cloakroom, where she collected her coat and put it on.

And just like on any other night she walked through the foyer.

There was a loud couple by the lifts who Gabi recognised as guests from the wedding and as she turned her head she saw a polished group coming in through the brass revolving doors.

No one was looking at Gabi.

The doors to the elevator were heavy and for a moment they did not budge and she wondered if he had forgotten to unlock them.

She was almost frantic, but suddenly they slid to one side and she stepped in and closed them.

His exotic fragrance lingered in the air and she leant against the soft cushioned wall.

The light was dim and she took a second, or

maybe ten, just to imprint this moment for, she knew, things between them could never be the same again.

Oh, she accepted this was just one night, but it would be the absolute night of her life and she would never regret it, Gabi swore.

She went to press the button but before she did so the elevator jolted, and she guessed Alim would have known she was inside and was impatient for her to arrive.

It *was* he who had pressed the summons.

For he *was* impatient.

Alim was an ordered person.

Even as the elevator lifted her towards him, he made plans. Tonight was not the time to offer her a position here at the hotel and as his lover; he would wait until tomorrow when his head was clearer.

For now, he would take her to the bedroom and make very slow love to her, for he knew she was inexperienced and deserved due care.

And for once there was tomorrow.

Yes, Alim made plans…but then he saw her. She was flushed in the face and her hands moved with his to open the gated doors. Their fingers met, and haste was born.

Gated elevators were not so good for self-control, for they started to kiss through the gates. Dirty, fevered kisses as their hands reached through the bars.

It was ridiculous—one second apart and they could open them and be together, but even a second apart felt too long.

For the greater good she stepped back as Alim

wrenched open the gate and rather than behaving shyly and reticently, as in her dreams she had been, she simply toppled into his arms.

How, he wondered, had he resisted her for so long?

'I hated it when you came up here with her...'

They were jealous words but she felt free to say them and he knew exactly the time Gabi referred to.

'You will recall that I sent her back down,' Alim said as he kissed her hard against the wall.

'Why?' she demanded.

'I was at risk of saying your name.'

'Why?'

'You know why,' Alim said, and mid-hallway, a long way from the entrance to his lounge, let alone the bedroom door, he recalled that incident. 'Because I was hard for you.'

He was hard for her now.

Her hands were in his hair and though she was unskilled in her kiss, so untamed and frantic was her mouth it was effort that was rewarded.

His hands dug hard into her bottom as they kissed; he felt her wriggle and Gabi let out an 'Ow' as he dug into her bruise.

'It's sore there,' she said, for all her senses felt heightened and she saw him frown in concern that he had hurt her. 'Where I fell,' she further explained.

Oh, yes.

His apartment might just as well be in Venice, for the corridor was simply too long for both of them; he would have to drag her, like a marathon runner across the finishing line. Oh, her determination was there but her willpower had gone at the same moment as his.

Still he kissed her hard against the wall, his tongue forcing apart her lips and his hands holding Gabi's wrists by her sides.

She ached to touch him, but he held her tight as he kissed her hard. Her arms attempted to flex, but his grip tightened and then suddenly released.

'Bed,' he said.

'Please,' she told him.

They fell through the door and were greeted by warmth and the scent of wood and pine and a fire lit in the grate.

It surprised Gabi, for she had expected opulence but not warmth.

He was behind her and the intention was bed but so warm was the room and so wanting the flesh that his hand came to her zipper.

'Show me where you hurt,' he said.

Gabi screwed her eyes closed for she wanted pitch blackness before she was naked but her dress was already sliding down.

She had felt beautiful in it, but now she was scared that the unwrapping of the parcel might reveal less than delicious contents.

Instead, she heard a low moan as he ran a finger down her spine.

'Alim…' Gabi breathed as she felt his fingers in her knickers, sliding them down.

Then he knelt and she felt his breath on her bottom

and then his mouth soft and warm, and she thought she might fold over.

Her thighs were shaking as she stepped out of her knickers.

His hands splayed her thighs so that she stood in her lovely high heels with her legs spread a little apart. He kissed the sensitive flesh of her inner thigh, then kissed the new purple bruise and it was bliss, but a bliss that could not last, for either of them, for more was needed for such pleasure to be sustained.

He stood then, undid her bra and turned her around.

He was completely dressed.

As if he had just come in to check on his staff.

You could not tell he had been on his knees between her thighs.

'I feel at a disadvantage,' she admitted, for she was naked apart from her shoes.

'Yet you have the complete advantage,' Alim said, for she could bring him back to his knees if she so chose.

Instead, she took off her shoes.

They made her unsteady—or was that Alim?—for his eyes never left her face as he shrugged off his jacket.

Gabi stood perfectly still, yet her breath came in pants as if she had been sprinting. His fingers reached for a nipple, taking it between finger and thumb, and then he looked down. Gabi swallowed as he lowered his head and took a leisurely taste; to steady herself, her hand went for his head.

But he removed it.

Her breast was wet and cool from his mouth as he removed his tie and shirt.

Oh, she had wanted to see him for so long. His skin was like burnt caramel and his chest was wide, his arms strong. She looked at the fan of hair and the dark puckered skin of his nipples, and she too wanted her taste. For a moment she resisted, for there were other feasts to be had.

She ran a hand along his upper arm and it was an unexpected move for Alim but he liked the soft touch of her hands and the slight pinch of her fingers.

Then she looked down at the snake of hair and the swell beneath and she bit on her lip because she knew tonight was going to hurt.

'I'll be gentle.'

'Really?'

And there was a dry edge to her voice, a smoky provocative edge that even Gabi had not heard in herself before.

She was stroking the crinkle of hair on his stomach and then her mouth went to his flat nipple; she licked the salty skin and this time it was Alim who held her head and moaned at the soft nip of her teeth. And it was Gabi who slid down his zipper.

Alim had anticipated reticence, yet her touch was eager.

They both stood naked now, so there was no disadvantage, not a single one.

She could see and feel and touch his desire, which

she did, stroking him at first then abandoning him erect so that she could reclaim his kiss.

He was damp and hard against her stomach and she was burning on the inside. She had dreamed of being kissed on his bed.

Instead, they did not make it past the fire.

They knelt, though their mouths remained engaged, sharing hot, wet kisses as they sank back onto their heels. His body was magnificent, his shoulders were wide as she ran her hands over them.

Always, she had felt cumbersome.

Not tonight.

He felt her lips stretch into a smile.

'What?' he asked, and pulled his head back a fraction.

'You always make me want to sit up straighter.'

'Sit up straighter, then.'

She had to fight to do so because, as he traced her clavicle with his tongue, she wanted to fold in two. Then down to her breast and he tasted it again, only slowly and deeply while massaging the other, rolling the swollen nipple between finger and thumb.

'Sit up straight,' he warned, as she started to sink into his skilled caress, which crept lower and lower.

She rested her arms on his shoulders as his fingers slipped into her tight hollow; she let out a sob of both pain and pleasure as he stretched and probed her, readying her for him.

She could sit up straight no more so he laid her down on the floor, stroking her and kissing her all the while.

His fingers did not rush, though his hand was insistent.

She went to push it away at one point for he made her want to scream, but instead Gabi clenched her jaw. He spoke in Arabic and his words, though not understood, matched her urgent desire.

He was passionate, sensual and far from cold as he coached her those final steps home.

'Come,' he told her, licking his lips, and she felt that if she did not then his lips would ensure that she did. Gabi succumbed to the pleasure, simply letting go.

She was tight around his fingers as her thighs clamped and her bottom lifted. Watching her pleasure was intense for Alim, and he fought his urgent need to take her.

Alim too was breathless as she lay there, temporarily sated, her hand over her mound.

She had not lied as others had, for there was blood on his fingers as he removed them.

Now they would retreat to the bedroom, yet still his hand roamed her thighs. Unwittingly, Gabi parted them for him, her mouth awaiting his kiss.

He fought with temptation and lost.

A little way, he decided, because he ached for her.

'It's going to hurt,' Gabi said, torn between fear and desire.

'A little,' he accepted, but despite his size her wetness eased him in.

It was *nothing* like her imaginings.

In her dreams it was a seamless, tender dance as he gently took her while telling her he loved her. In reality it was the tearing of flesh and the rising of pain as he inched into her.

Gabi found that she preferred the latter.

'Gabi…'

He had sworn *just a little way in*, but the grip was too inviting, the scent of sex urged him on and he thrust in deeply.

She sobbed, loudly, and he cursed his lack of care. Alim stilled. It took a moment for her to acclimatise, to regroup, and then she begged him to do it again.

Alim obliged.

Over and over.

They rolled and they kissed, they dragged from each other pleasure beyond imagining, and she, the virgin, pushed him to extremes, for he fought hard not to come.

His life, his identity, even his seed was always protected.

Yet his abdomen was tight and he was lifting.

He did not withdraw and she did not resist. Instead, she coiled her legs tighter around his loins, and this time, when Gabi came, it was around his thick length.

He felt the throb of her demand.

'Alim…' Her voice told him *now*, in fact it pleaded, and Alim bade farewell to restraint and rained deep into her.

The rush of his release and the moan he made procured a tiny cry from Gabi that abruptly died, for she was back to his mouth, being consumed by his kiss and a slave to their bliss.

They lay there a while, until both the room and their bodies were cool. But the fires of passion had not dimmed.

'Bed,' Alim said, and he stood and helped her up.

For still it beckoned.

CHAPTER SIX

ALIM HAD ALWAYS been careful.

Always!

Until now.

There was nothing about this night that compared with others, for they made love again and then, instead of sleeping, lay in his bed, talking, thirstily drinking iced sparkling water.

It was refreshing.

Even mistakes were forgiven.

'Tomorrow I shall arrange for a doctor to see you,' he told Gabi as they discussed the morning-after pill.

'I'll sort it,' Gabi said, for she was not seeing a doctor here!

'I apologise,' he told her.

'Please don't.'

She would not change it, or, if she could, Gabi would only have been better prepared and been on the Pill, but nothing could have forewarned her that on this night her dreams would come true.

She had craved Alim from a distance for years.

Now he was here and it was better even than she had dreamt.

Gabi might be inexperienced but she knew enough about Alim to be surprised by their ease in conversation afterwards.

She had known that he would be a brilliant lover; the surprise was that afterwards she felt like she was lying with a friend, for they chatted.

And she had never imagined that might happen with Alim.

Yet they spoke about their lack of thought earlier and made plans to remedy it later that day.

'I will sort it,' she told him. 'Believe me, I have no intention of ending up like—' She halted.

'Like who?'

'My mother,' Gabi said. 'I don't mean that I don't want to be like her, I mean I don't want to resent…'

Whatever way she said it made it sound wrong.

'Tell me,' Alim said, just as he had when they had spoken outside the ballroom, only this time she was wrapped in his arms.

'I was an accident,' Gabi explained. 'One she still pays for to this day.'

'Surely not,' Alim said. 'What about your father?'

'I don't know who he is.' Gabi admitted. 'It doesn't matter, I don't need to know…'

But she did.

Often, the need to know was so acute that she could not bear it, yet she played it down as she always had.

'My mother had been accepted to study at university but had to give it up to raise me.'

'It is not your fault that she did not follow her dreams.'

'It feels like it,' Gabi admitted. 'If she hadn't had me...'

'Then she would have found another excuse.'

'That's harsh,' Gabi said.

'Perhaps,' Alim conceded, and he smiled as she looked at him.

'Are you always so direct?'

'Always.'

Now it was Gabi who smiled.

'So planning weddings is your dream?' he asked.

Gabi nodded. She told him about when she had been a little girl and the flour and sugar that had driven her mother wild. 'I would pick flowers at the park for the bouquet and spend the whole day making sure that everything was perfect.' She thought for a moment. 'I was so worried about this wedding. It was so incredibly rushed but when I saw James and Mona dance last night I knew that they'd be okay.'

'How did you know that?'

'You can tell,' Gabi said. 'She was a very difficult bride, but together they seem so happy.'

He liked hearing that, for Alim wanted happiness for his brother.

It was not something he sought for himself.

Alim did not believe in happy marriages. He had been raised with the model that marriage was a business arrangement and a duty, and that happiness was sought elsewhere.

Things were different, of course, for James for he did not have the burden of being his father's heir.

Yes, he admitted in that moment, at times it felt like a burden.

Night was fading but there was no real thought of sleeping as they lay together chatting, Gabi idly running her fingers in circles on his chest.

And for Alim it was very relaxing, too, as well as a bit of a turn-on. He liked her curiosity about his body and her conversation made him smile as she moaned about Bernadetta, and the hell of getting this wedding sorted. But then Gabi crossed the line.

'The groom's mother is paying.'

'Gabi!' he scolded.

'What?'

Alim was considering her for a very senior role, yet she dropped confidential information like a shower of rain.

'You should not discuss such things.'

'Oh, come on,' Gabi said. 'I'm not down at the bar talking about it, I'm in bed with the boss. And it's you she's paying, so you must already know.' And then she smiled and it was like a rainbow and Alim found himself smiling back.

'Okay,' he conceded, and he pulled her in so that she lay with her head on his chest.

'It *is* odd, though,' Gabi said, though she was more thinking out loud, and it was so easy to do so with his hand stroking her hair. 'Usually it's the bride's parents who pay, or half and half…'

Alim shrugged. 'Perhaps Mona's parents are not wealthy.'

'Perhaps.' Gabi yawned. 'Though Fleur clearly is. She intrigues me.'

'Who?'

'Fleur,' Gabi said. 'The mother of the groom.'

Alim said nothing.

'I can't work out if she's divorced or widowed or just single like my mother.'

'Does it matter?' Alim asked.

'Probably not.'

Of course it did, Alim thought. Or it soon would.

He knew how the staff gossiped and very soon Gabi would know his title and it would be clear that the royal guests in residence tonight were related to him.

Or perhaps it would be the wedding photos that would be his undoing when Gabi saw them, for they had made love now and had stared deep into each other's eyes.

Alim knew he was a darker version of James.

Gabi might well see it too.

She was perceptive enough that soon she might work things out.

Alim did not enlighten her now, though.

There would be time for all that tomorrow.

It was more than one night he wanted, yet he was aware that he needed to think things through carefully.

And anyway, for now, Gabi was sleeping.

The more he tried to talk himself out of the plans he was making, the more sense they made. With his father unwell, the months ahead would be trying—that much Alim knew.

He could not put off marriage for ever, but he could certainly delay things.

And what nicer delay than this?

Alim did not expect Gabi to be at his beck and call as he carried on in the usual way; he would be faithful.

A year, perhaps.

It would work for both of them.

Alim's assessment was based on practicalities. Away from Bernadetta, her career would only flourish, he would see to that. And, during this difficult year, he could come back to Rome and to Gabi. There would be no scandal for the palace to deal with, particularly when he began taking a more prominent role while his father sought treatment.

Alim was arrogant enough to assume that Gabi would have no issues with what he was about to propose; after all, women never said no to him, and he was offering more to Gabi then he had to any woman in his life before.

Aside from his commitment to his country, it was the biggest pledge he had made and Alim made it in the still of the night as she lay sleeping.

The sky was grey and silver as the sun rose on a very cold Rome and he thought of her dress on the floor in another room and the soft warm body he held.

Gabi felt the roam of his hands as she awoke and turned her face for a glimpse of Alim asleep but it was denied to her, for Alim was already awake and looking at her.

He watched her eyes flicker open and her face turn to him. He wondered if he would see a grimace or a startle of panic as she recalled their night, but instead he watched as a smile stretched her lips and her sleepy eyes met his.

'Best night,' she said.

It had been.

And those were exactly the words he wanted to hear, for there was no tinge of regret in her smile and no confusion in her eyes.

Only desire.

And Alim *still* felt the same.

During the hours Gabi had slept, Alim had been thinking.

Yes, he still wanted more than one night.

'Fleur did not pay for the wedding,' he said, and watched her frown at the odd choice of topic, wrapped as they were in each other's arms and a breath away from a deep morning kiss.

She did not get yet that this was the most intimate conversation in the whole of Alim's life.

'It was my gift to Mona and James.'

'Why?'

'Because James is my half-brother.'

Her frown deepened and she ran a tongue over

her lips as she tried to work things out; now that he had said it, she could see that James and Alim were related.

Gabi had started to see that last night as she had watched the couple dance—or rather there had been something in James that had spoken to her.

Now that she knew, Gabi felt almost foolish that she had not seen it more readily.

'Fleur is my father's mistress,' Alim explained.

'I don't understand,' Gabi said.

'Listen to me.' Alim's eyes and his tone told her that what he was saying was very important. 'Fleur was my father's lover but his father did not consider her a suitable bride. When she got pregnant with James, my grandfather summoned my father home and arranged his marriage to my mother, even though my father loved Fleur.'

'Why did he agree to marry a woman if he loved another?'

'Because he had little choice. His father was the Sultan of Sultans and his word is law; now that title belongs to my father.'

He actually felt the goose-bumps rise on her arm. 'And so what does that make you?'

'A sultan, and one day I shall rule.'

'Why are you telling me this?'

'Because my father is here in the hotel and it won't be long before the staff work out our connection. Soon you would have too.'

'But why are you telling me now?' she persisted.

'Because things back home are changing. My father is unwell, so I am going to have to travel there a lot in the coming months…' Still she stared at him with a puzzled look in her eyes so he made things a little clearer. 'I want to spend more time with you when I am here in Rome. Last night I was going to ask you to work for me as the events co-ordinator at the Grande Lucia.'

It was the offer of a lifetime.

Stunning, in fact.

It was the gateway to a shiny future and, Gabi realised, she may well have blown it for one night in his bed.

But still, she thought, she would not change it for anything.

'Is that offer being reconsidered in the light of certain events?' Gabi asked.

He smiled. 'It is being amended.'

And seriously so.

'What about a one-year contract?' he said.

'One year?'

'That frees you from Bernadetta; you would make many contacts here during that time.'

'And is sleeping with me a part of that contract?'

'Gabi.' Alim heard her indignation but was calm in his response. 'I think from last night it is clear we are not going to be able to work together and keep things strictly business. Of course, we will be discreet in front of the staff but…'

'You've really got this all worked out, haven't you?'

'I've given it considerable thought, yes.'

Gabi had walked in here last night without a doubt that it would be over by the morning.

Certain of it.

Reassured by it, in fact.

For Alim was a self-confessed reprobate and her heart could not be dangled on elastic by him, waiting to be hauled to his bedroom one minute, ignored or discarded the next.

She was shaken, seriously so.

'What happens when someone else comes along?'

She was direct with her questions and he liked that.

'Alim, I take my career seriously...'

'And I admire that you do,' he responded. 'I shan't mess with it. And,' he offered, which for Alim was a great concession, 'there will be no one else.'

'Why a year?'

'Because I will be called home to marry.'

How cruel that he held her as he said that.

'Gabi.' He had felt her stiffen. 'Please, listen to me now. When Fleur fell pregnant my grandfather invoked a pre-marital diktat on my father. It is a harsh law, one intended to bring a reluctant groom to heel. Once invoked there can be no lovers, save for in the desert.'

'The desert?' she asked. 'You mean a harem.'

'That is what it meant then; they could have worked around it, but Fleur refused to be his desert mistress.'

'I don't blame her for that.'

'By the time James was due to be born my mother was pregnant with me. Fleur gave birth in London; my father could not leave at the time. But later, once he had royal heirs, things were easier for them and my father was more free to travel…'

Gabi didn't want to hear it. She sat up and clutched the sheet around her 'This conversation is medieval.' She did not like what she was hearing—it unnerved her, in fact—but Alim calmly spoke on.

'Perhaps when you see the doctor this morning you should speak about going on the Pill. I can call and arrange for him to see you here…'

'I make my own appointments, Alim, and I don't need to be told what to ask for.' She shot him a look. 'I don't need to go on the Pill because I'm not going to be your mistress…'

'Lover,' Alim corrected, for they were two very different roles.

'I am not going to be your lover for a year until your father summons you home.'

'I have given it a lot of thought.'

'Have you, now?'

'I don't see the issue.'

'Your assumption, for a start.'

She got out of bed and headed for the shower.

Gabi was sore from last night and her head was whirling from all she had been told.

And he was wrong about not messing with careers, Gabi thought as she showered.

Wrapping a towel around her, she headed out and told him so.

'What about Marianna? She's given the Grande Lucia years of her life and you'd discard her like that.' She tried to snap wet fingers; it didn't work.

'She wants to wind down her hours,' Alim answered. 'I would offer her a consulting role.'

She looked at him and for a brief second he seemed not so ruthless but then his hand shot out, stripping off the towel, and she stood naked. He would be ruthless to her heart, she amended.

But her body craved him.

It would be foolish at best not to go on the Pill because all she wanted at this moment was to climb back into bed.

'I know it's a lot to take in,' Alim said. 'But at least give it some thought.'

He did not understand her anger; most women pleaded for more time with him after all. 'Would you prefer it to have been just a one-night stand?'

'Yes.' She actually laughed—somewhat incredulously. 'Yes,' she said again, for this was too much for her to deal with.

'Liar.'

She caught his eyes and her laughter died. Gabi swallowed, because he actually meant it, she was starting to realise.

No!

'A year at your bidding?' she mocked.

'It works both ways,' Alim responded. 'I would be at your bidding too.'

He watched the colour spread up her cheeks and across her chest as she attempted indignation. He watched as she stood to pull on her knickers then sat back down to put on her bra.

He sat up and did it up for her and then kissed the back of her neck.

His tongue was thorough and he moved so he sat naked behind Gabi and kissed her neck harder as his hands played with her breasts.

'Alim.'

She was hot in the face and unable to stand and he knew it. Now one hand came down and slipped into her knickers. She was sore and swollen from last night, and his fingers were not there with the intent to soothe.

This love would hurt.

And it would be love, it possibly already was, but a year at his beck and call would only cement that fact.

'Alim…' She wanted to turn in his arms, to wrap herself around him, but he just upped the beats of pressure and kept bruising her neck with his mouth as she came.

And then he released her.

Somehow Gabi stood.

'The offer's there,' he told her.

And the pleasure might have been hers, but Alim knew it had been worth the restraint from him, for now they ached for each other.

It was the greatest feat of her life to dress and

leave, yet she needed the ice of the winter morning just to learn how to breathe again, and somehow think.

But the confusion he'd spun her into was not yet complete.

Alim leant over and opened a drawer to his beside.

The rumours were true, for there, in a small dish, as one might display after-dinner mints, was a collection of diamonds.

They sparkled in the wintry light, they beguiled, and one alone could make the months ahead so much easier for Gabi.

'Choose one,' Alim said. 'And then tomorrow—'

'I shan't be your whore.'

'In my country the tradition is—'

'We're in Rome, Alim,' she interrupted, and her lips pressed together in anger. Gabi shot him a look and then walked into the lounge and straight to her purse.

He made her feel confident. She felt emboldened.

Somehow he gave her permission to be completely herself.

And that self was cross!

'Here…' She opened up her purse and emptied the entire contents onto the bed. It wasn't much—a lot of coins and a few notes—but she tipped them all out and made him the whore now. 'Treat yourself, baby,' Gabi said.

As she walked out, to the surprise of both of them, Alim laughed.

He never laughed, and certainly not in the morning, yet here he was doing just that.

And, as the door slammed, Alim knew but one thing.

He wanted her back in his bed.

CHAPTER SEVEN

'THE SULTAN OF SULTANS is ready to receive you.'

Alim thanked Violetta when she called to inform him that his father was finally ready for him.

He had showered and dressed in black linen trousers and a fitted white shirt and then impatiently awaited the summons.

Alim had been looking forward to breakfast with the newlyweds, to being able to speak more freely with them.

Now, though, he was also looking forward to the rest of the day.

To the upcoming year.

He knew he had overwhelmed Gabi and that it was all too much to take in, but once she had thought it through, Alim was certain there was hope for them.

Alim looked forward not just to the nights ahead but to the working days, for he had loved this hotel on sight. Shabby, cheaply renovated, he had poured much into it and breathed it back to life. With Gabi as the new functions co-ordinator there was much to look forward to on many levels.

Violetta was waiting outside the Royal Suite. She gave Alim a smile as he approached, then three short knocks on the door to announce Alim's arrival. He opened it and stepped in, expecting to greet his family, but instead there was only his father.

'Alim.' Oman's voice was not particularly welcoming.

'Where are James and Mona?' Alim asked once he had bowed.

'On their way to Paris,' Oman said. 'I asked that they join me a little earlier.'

'I am sure they would have appreciated the early morning call the day after their wedding.'

Sarcasm was wasted on his father, Alim knew.

Still, he had long since realised that if he wanted a relationship with James then he had to forge that for himself.

When Alim had found out he had a half-brother, instead of quietly ignoring it, as would have been his parents' preferred way of dealing with things, Alim had insisted that they meet.

He had kept alive the relationship with his brother with calls, messages and visits, and would continue to do so. Once the newlyweds were back in Rome, Alim would see them, or he might call in a few days and catch up with them in Paris.

It would be good to see Kaleb too.

'What about Yasmin?' Alim asked.

'Violetta told me that she is unwell,' Oman said. 'Apparently she has a migraine—too much excitement last night.'

Or too much champagne, Alim thought, but made no comment as his father spoke on. 'It is just as well for I wish to speak to you alone. With all I told you last night there is a lot to discuss.'

'Very well.'

A gleaming walnut table had been laid and a feast prepared. Alim looked over to where it stood waiting on a large silver trolley.

There were no staff present, Alim noted, as was the case when formal business was to be discussed.

Alim was not really in the mood for a breakfast briefing but given his father's illness he knew there would be a lot to sort out.

If they'd been in Zethlehan, there might be an elder present in case sensitive issues were raised, but for now it was just the two of them.

Alim first served his father and then himself.

Oman preferred fruit, and usually so too did Alim, but this morning he helped himself to a generous serving of *shakshuka*—baked eggs in a rich and spicy sauce. There were several chefs at the Grande Lucia, including two from Zethlehan that Alim had brought over. He made light conversation with his father as he sat down.

'The Middle Eastern brunch at this hotel is becoming increasingly popular. Now people have to book in advance.'

Oman made no comment; he did not approve of Alim having investments overseas, and he particularly loathed his son's passion for this one.

And then Oman said it.

He did not look up; he said it as easily as he might ask for more mint tea.

'For some time now I have been considering invoking the pre-marital diktat.'

Alim, who had anticipated many things for the year ahead, had never envisaged this.

Never.

His father loathed the diktat, since it had been forced upon him, and Alim could not believe that he would bring this harsh ruling to bear on his son.

'There is no need for that.' Alim kept his voice calm, though he was rarely unsettled.

'It would seem that there is. I have been asking to choose your bride for many years.'

'And I have told you—' Alim's voice was still silk, but laced with threat '—that I shall never be pushed into marriage.'

Alim stared at his father. Not only was this unexpected, it was vindictive. 'You loathe that diktat,' Alim pointed out.

'It has its merits. My father chose well for me—your mother is an exemplary queen and our people adore her. We have raised three heirs...'

'And you hate it that you could not marry Fleur.' He'd said her name out loud.

Now was not the time for reticence.

'You hate that your first born bears no title and that the woman you love gets no recognition.' Alim tried to stare down his father but Oman refused to meet his glare. 'You cannot do this.'

'It is done,' Oman told him. 'I informed the elders this morning. As of now you are Sultan Elect.'

This meant Alim was a sultan in choosing.

From this point on he must remain celibate for he could bring no shame on any future bride. There could be no release save from discreet times in the desert.

Alim stood, his appetite totally gone.

'You cannot force me into marriage.'

He said it again, loudly this time, and Alim never shouted.

Ever.

But this morning he did.

Oman did not flinch. In fact, vindictive had been the right word to describe his father's mood for the Sultan of Sultans' smile was black when he offered his response.

'I can make single life hell for you, though. You've had your fun, Alim. It's time to grow up.'

A year.

Gabi had stamped her way home through the slush and cold, furious at his suggestion.

But her flat was cold when she entered and she thought of the warmth she had left and the bliss of last night.

It should be over with by now.

Right now, Gabi thought, she should be accepting that, though amazing, her time with Alim was done.

Yet her mind danced with the hope of more.

Even before she had made a quick coffee, Bernadetta called.

'I have a meeting with a bride this afternoon but my vertigo has come on and I'm not going to be able to get there…'

Gabi closed her eyes as Bernadetta dragged out one of her tired excuses.

'Can it be moved to tomorrow?' Gabi asked.

Aside from all that had happened with Alim, Gabi had worked through to midnight and still had a lot to get done today.

She had to take the gramophone and record back to the grandparents, which was a considerable drive, and there were the outfits to collect, and a hundred other jobs that would go unnoticed but ensured that yesterday's wedding was seamless for the family.

'I don't want to let down a prospective client,' Bernadetta said. 'Gabi, I really haven't got the energy for debate. It's a summer wedding to be held at the Grande Lucia; you're going to be there today anyway.'

'I don't have a suit,' Gabi reminded her boss. 'Bernadetta…' Gabi paused. She was about to say no to her, Gabi realised. She had been about to stand up to Bernadetta and not just on the strength of Alim's offer this morning. Their conversation last night had resonated. She was tired of being pushed around and knew she was worth a whole lot more than the treatment Bernadetta served, but for now Gabi held her tongue.

Her next step required careful thought, and so, instead of standing her ground, Gabi brushed down her skirt and did the best repair job that she could on the torn seam of her jacket and then headed back to the Grande Lucia.

There was a lot of activity in the foyer as huge brass trolleys filled with expensive luggage were being moved out.

'Gabi!'

She turned and smiled when she saw that it was the photographer. 'How did things go with you last night?' Gabi asked.

'Probably not as well as you,' he said, and Gabi frowned as he held out one of his cameras. 'I left this running in the gallery,' he explained. 'I set it to take intermittent photos up until midnight.'

Now Gabi started to blush as she realised what might have been captured.

He held out the camera and Gabi could almost not bring herself to look at the screen, terrified what she might see. 'Not exactly part of the bridal package, though it's a very beautiful image.' The photographer said.

Oh, yet another gaffe! Gabi thought, cringing, but she forced herself to look.

And then all the magic of last night returned.

For it had been captured exquisitely.

On the stunning ballroom floor, there, swirling in Alim's arms, was Gabi.

It was as beautiful as any professional wedding photo, though it was almost impossible to reconcile that this was their first night and that they had at that point not so much as kissed.

She knew the very second that the photo had been

taken. It had been when Alim had warned her that he was trouble and she had lifted her face to his.

The moment had been captured perfectly, for she was looking up into his eyes and Alim was holding her tenderly but firmly.

'Would you like me to delete it?' the photographer checked.

'No.'

'I thought as much.'

They had worked together on many occasions and he had Gabi's contact details. 'I'll forward it to you.'

He headed off with all his equipment and Gabi wanted to call out to him not to forget to forward it, but instead Gabi caught sight of Fleur in one of the side lounges, giving her order to a maid.

The woman had always intrigued Gabi, but never more so than now.

Was it lonely to be Fleur? Gabi pondered.

Of course it must be, but Alim wasn't suggesting the same for her. This was a business plan almost, a manageable slice of time.

A year.

She said it again to herself, though with mounting excitement this time.

Gabi had never dated, but knew from her friends that most relationships didn't even last that long.

It was the way he had said it and the assumption that she would simply comply that had irked.

'Gabi!' Anya, the receptionist on today, called out to her, and as Gabi looked over she realised that the

foyer had become very busy. 'Can I ask you to step
back, please? We have some VIP's about to leave.'

'Sure.'

Some dark-suited men were walking through the
foyer and Gabi knew they were the hotel's security.

And she was about to see the Sultan of Sultans,
Gabi realised.

She watched as the entourage moved through the
foyer.

There was a young woman with a long mane of
black hair wearing a deep mustard-coloured velvet
gown and jewelled slippers. She was very beautiful,
Gabi thought, even if her eyes were hidden behind
dark glasses.

And then she saw a man dressed in a robe of black
with a silver *keffiyeh* and Gabi felt her breath burn as
she held it in her lungs, for she knew it was Alim's
father. He was a mature version of Alim and had the
same air of authority and elegance.

The managing director was in the foyer to bid
farewell to the royal guests.

Usually, of course, it would be the owner.

Except the owner happened to be his son.

It all made sense now.

Fleur's insistence on the venue, and the reason
that there had been few guests on the groom's side.

And all too soon it was over.

The procession walked through the foyer and out
to the waiting cars, and when the last of them had
gone, Gabi looked over to the lounge and to Fleur,

who sat dignified and straight but terribly, terribly alone.

Gabi watched as she reached into her purse and took out a handkerchief, pressing it to her lips for a moment to gather herself.

There had been no kiss goodbye, not even so much as a glance aimed at her by the Sultan of Sultans. No public acknowledgement from the man to whom she had borne a son.

What Alim had proposed this morning was different, though, Gabi told herself.

It was a year of her life and until last night there had been no love life for her.

It had been work, work, work.

Which she loved, of course.

But for a year she could have both.

And then what?

She saw that Fleur was making her way to the elevators and for the first time Gabi saw this usually poised woman with her shoulders slumped.

Defeated.

But that would not happen to her, Gabi assured herself, for she knew exactly what she was getting into. And Alim himself had said she would be a lover rather than a mistress. She had been carrying a flame for Alim since she had first seen him; the difference now was that she would be not carrying it alone.

And then?

She could not think of that now.

She was going to say yes.

It hadn't taken days of consideration, just hours,

to come to her decision, and now that she had, hope filled her heart.

And as if in answer to her decision she watched as the gated, private elevator that had taken her to his suite last night opened.

Alim stepped out and her heart squeezed in reaction.

He was clean shaven and immaculate. But instead of ignoring Fleur, as he had before, Gabi watched as he stood and spoke for a moment with the woman and the conversation appeared tense.

It was.

'I tried to stop him, Alim,' Fleur said, 'but we both know my word holds little sway.'

And Alim let out a mirthless laugh for he had just come off the phone with his mother, imploring her to try and change Oman's mind, but her response had been almost the same.

'You hold more sway than you know,' Alim said. 'You simply refuse to stand up to him.'

'You try, then!' Fleur said, and her voice was weary.

Oh, he would.

Alim respected his father's title but not always the man himself.

Yet he was the ruler and his word was law.

Alim had tried to tell himself that just because the diktat had been invoked it did not mean that *everything* had to change. He would take over more duties while his father had treatment, but his work could continue here. Then he saw Gabi, standing in the foyer, dressed in that awful suit, but now that he had bedded her, she looked more beautiful than ever before and he realised that *everything* had changed.

The true ramifications were starting to hit home.

It was not even just about sex, for there could be no intimate conversation, no working alongside a woman for whom he harboured such thoughts.

And perhaps, more pointedly, no hope of observing the laws when Gabi was around.

He could only hope that her mood with him was as dark as it had been when she had left his bed this morning, so there would be no need to speak.

Alim could only think in minutes at the moment, so he focussed on getting through the next few and, ignoring her gaze, he walked across the foyer. He wanted to be outside and to walk the streets of Rome.

He had changed his mind by the time he reached the brass doors, for Alim did not, by nature, avoid issues. He turned and walked towards Gabi, and when he saw her smile Alim knew she was going to say yes to the chance for them.

He watched the smile die on her lips as he approached.

'That offer…' Alim said, and he hesitated. He had been right when he'd said it would be impossible to work alongside each other and not sleep together.

'Yes?'

Here was no place to explain the diktat, but they could not be alone. He thought of her in bed this morning, wrapping the sheet around herself when he had tried to explain the rules and how lovers could only be alone in the desert.

Medieval had been her word to describe it.

It would be kinder to simply end it now, Alim knew.

It was also necessary.

He could smell the slight apple scent of her shampoo and could see the soft swelling of her mouth, a remnant from last night's hot kisses. He thought of how swollen she had been in readiness for him, and he thought of the love they could so easily still make.

Their bodies were aware of each other, they were attuned and wanting but, as of this morning, they were forbidden.

And so he said it, simply ended any hope for them.

'The offer has been withdrawn.'

He watched the colour drain from her face. He watched her rapid blink, and there was nothing he could do to comfort her.

'I see,' Gabi said, even though she didn't.

Yet she fought for dignity.

And dignity felt like a trapeze that she must grab onto, only Gabi was no acrobat.

She had only just accepted hope, only just accepted the brief possibility of them, and now it had been snatched away.

By him.

Oh, she had known he would hurt her one day, but after the way he had treated her that morning Gabi had never thought it would be today.

She could not even ask why or demand an explanation for she was fighting not to break down. Her nails dug into her palms and her breath was so shallow it made her feel a little giddy.

'You'll take care of what we discussed?' Alim checked.

Gabi looked at him. He was a bastard to the core, she decided, for she would have happily settled for just one night, but he'd ruined that with the glimpse of a dream. So as the imaginary trapeze swung by, she grabbed onto it with one hand and hoped it would quickly carry her away from him and drop her where she could weep unseen.

'Of course,' she responded.

'Gabi...' His voice husked and he did not continue with whatever it was he had been about to say.

It was Gabi who filled the silence. 'I need to get on,' she said. 'Bernadetta has given me quite a list to get through today.'

And she completed it. Somehow she got through the first day. Gabi and Marianna met with the new bride-to-be and her mother.

'We have the last Saturday in July available,' Marianna informed them.

'No, I want August,' the bride-to-be said.

'I'm sorry.' Marianna shook her head. 'Summer weddings have to be booked a long way in advance.'

'It's more than six months away!' the bride insisted.

'You are lucky that we have this one available.'

And Gabi just sat there.

Usually she would make soothing noises to take the edge off Marianna's slightly scolding tone.

She had been about to throw in her job, Gabi thought in horror. So trusting had she been that she had almost given Bernadetta her notice.

The numbness was fading, replaced now by a burn of anger as she watched Alim walk through the foyer.

Elegant, beautiful, it looked as if he had not a care in the world.

The rumours were true. Cold and callous did suit him. Alim did not look in her direction. She had been, Gabi knew, dismissed from his life.

And then the anger faded as she began to feel bereft. Soon followed by fear.

CHAPTER EIGHT

GABI DID NOT take care of things as the Sultan had ordered.

Though not out of recklessness or spite.

The first few days had felt like a bereavement, though not one she could ring in to work and explain about.

What could she say? *Bernadetta, I slept with Alim and he promised me the world and then dumped me.*

At best, she was a fool to have believed at all. Yet his behaviour made no sense to Gabi, for he had not offered her anything in the heat of passion. It had all been in the calm coolness of the morning, after hours of thinking, he had said.

So Gabi had somehow remembered to breathe as she'd fought not to cry and had done her best to get on with her work.

And by the time the fog had if not lifted then parted enough to take care of anything other than the seconds ahead, she had gone to the *farmacia*, only to find out that she had left it too late.

Late.

It became her most used word.

She was a day late, but put it down to stress.

A week late, but that happened at times.

And then she was late for work two days in a row because even the scent of her favourite morning coffee had her hunched over the bathroom sink.

Terror was her new friend.

Not just that she was pregnant, but by whom.

The more she found out about Zethlehan and the more she discovered about the power of the royals there, the more acute her terror became.

'Pregnant?'

'Yes,' Gabi had said to her mother.

It was a gorgeous spring morning.

Gabi had come from a weekend at the stunning Castelli vineyard, where the wedding had gone off beautifully, and she had told herself it was time. It had taken three months for Gabi to finally find the courage to tell her mother.

'Who is the father?' Carmel had asked.

And when Gabi had not answered, her mother had slapped her cheek.

Carmel, herself a single mother, had never wanted the same struggle for her only child.

'There go your dreams,' Carmel had said.

'No.'

Gabi knew things would be difficult but she was determined that her dreams would continue. It was her lack of contact with Alim that felt like an insufferable loss.

She had not told him about the baby.

Her mother assumed that because Gabi did not say who the father of her child was, it meant that she did not know.

Now Gabi was almost glad that she had been unable to tell Alim.

She was scared.

Not so much of his reaction, more the repercussions.

Sultan Alim of Zethlehan.

Sultan Elect.

He was next in line to the throne and the more she read about his kingdom the more she feared him. Alim was more powerful than she could fathom. His country was rich, extremely prosperous, and the royalty adored. There was a brother and a sister. Alim was the eldest and one day he would be Sultan of Sultans.

Gabi did not know how an illegitimate baby would be dealt with.

Her only reference point was Fleur, and she would never allow herself to become her, Gabi swore.

Though perhaps she was doing Alim an injustice?

On several occasions, Gabi had walked past the Grande Lucia, trying to find the courage to go in. Sometimes she would speak with Ronaldo and pretend that she was merely passing.

A couple of times she had plucked up the courage to go in but now Alim's royal status was known, security around him was tighter.

'Is Alim here?' Gabi asked Anya.

'Do you have an appointment?' Anya checked,

when once she would have simply nodded or shaken her head, or picked up the phone to alert him.

'No,' Gabi said. 'I don't.'

'Then I can see if Marianna is available.'

'It's fine.' Gabi shook her head and, turning, looked over to the lounge and thought of Fleur, sitting alone and unacknowledged, and she thought too of James.

She did not want that life for her child, though it probably wasn't even an option to them. The Sultan of Sultans loved Fleur, whereas Alim had coldly ended things the morning after a night in his bed.

He had also told her to take the morning-after pill, not once, not twice, but three times.

Gabi was scared but determined to cope, for now, alone.

And so the next person she had told was Bernadetta.

And Bernadetta's reaction had been one of pure spite.

She resented that she would be paying for maternity leave and decided to get her money's worth while she could.

Every wedding that Bernadetta could, she passed over to Gabi.

Each teary bride or stressed call from the mother of said bride, Gabi dealt with.

And the most recent couple had barely left the church before Bernadetta skived off. Gabi barely had time to think, she was so busy working as Bernadetta became increasingly demanding.

'I don't want you showing,' she said when Gabi asked about wearing a dress for work rather than the hated suit.

It was the middle of summer and the weight had fallen off Gabi—or rather she had not, to her doctor's concern, put any on. Always curvy, at close to seven months pregnant she barely showed, but that wasn't good enough for Bernadetta.

'Our clients want to think your mind is on the job, not on a baby.'

'It *is* on the job,' Gabi insisted.

But the heavy suit remained. The only concession was that she wore the cream cowl-necked top out of the waistband.

And concealing her pregnancy as best she could was perhaps wise, for all too soon it was the wedding at the Grande Lucia that she had taken on the day the bottom had fallen out of her world.

Not that Alim would notice her, and neither was she likely to see him.

He was barely around any more. Ronaldo had told her that he had moved back to Zethlehan and, sadly, the Grande Lucia was now on the market.

The staff were all worried for their jobs.

It was still beautiful, though, Gabi thought as, on the Friday before the wedding, she went for a breakfast meeting with Marianna in her office.

First they spoke about the timings of the big day and the arrival of the cars and photographers and such things.

Gabi's main focus was the wedding.

For Marianna, although the wedding was important, she was also dealing with the comfort of the other hotel guests and ensuring that they were not inconvenienced too much.

Again, Gabi pushed for a change to the flowers in the foyer.

'No, there has always been a red floral display.' Marianna shook her head and refused to budge on the issue. 'Our return guests like the familiarity.'

'But don't you want to attract new guests?'

Marianna pursed her lips as Gabi pushed on. 'Some of the hotels I work with actually organise in advance for their floral displays to tie in with the bridal theme…'

'The Grande Lucia does not compete with other hotels,' Marianna said. 'We're already at the top.'

Thanks to Alim, Gabi thought.

And Marianna was arrogant in her assumption that just because they were successful they could ignore competition.

For a very long while, before Alim had taken over, the hotel had struggled. Mona had been right in her description—the hotel had looked tired and many a potential bride had turned up her nose when the venue had been suggested. Oh, it was because of Alim that the Grande Lucia was now thriving and everyone knew it.

'I hear it will soon be under new ownership,' Gabi said.

'Yes, Alim is bringing potential buyers through over the weekend.'

'He's here?' Gabi squeaked, and then quickly recovered. Her voice had sounded too urgent, her words a demand, and she fought to relax herself. 'I thought that he was back in the Middle East?'

'For the most part he is there,' Marianna agreed. 'But this an important weekend. Today Signor Raul Di Savo is in residence and has free rein to look around; tomorrow it will be Signor Bastiano Conti.'

Gabi felt her heart sink a little. Hotels often took ages to sell but these were two serious names in the industry. Matrimoni di Bernadetta had held many weddings at Raul's boutique hotel here in Rome, and Gabi knew that Bastiano was also a formidable player in the industry.

'If you come across either of them, please be polite,' Marianna said.

'Of course.'

'They may have questions for you.'

Gabi nodded.

'And, please, ensure that all deliveries are discreet and that there is minimal disturbance to our guests. Alim is soon to marry so he wants the Grande Lucia off his hands as quickly as possible.'

Gabi just sat there.

She had read about it, of course, but it hurt to hear it voiced.

Even Alim had said that they could only last for a year because he had commitments back home.

How she wished they had had that year

Or maybe not, Gabi thought as she sat there, trying to fathom being closer to him than she had been that night, knowing him more, loving him more…

For, yes, despite the anger and pain, Gabi now knew that it was love.

At least on her side.

'Gabi?' Marianna frowned because it was clear their meeting was over yet Gabi had made no move to leave. 'Was there anything else?'

'I don't think so.'

There could be no hope for them.

It was a very busy day spent liaising with the florists and soothing a temperamental head chef when she informed him that there had been some last-minute food preferences called in.

'I already have the updated list,' he told her.

'No,' Gabi said. 'There are more.'

A lot more.

And the head chef was not happy, declaring, as if it were her fault, that the world had gone gluten-free.

The gowns and outfits arrived and it was for Gabi to organise that tomorrow they would be sent to the correct suites.

She spoke with the make-up artist and hairdressers too, ensuring that every detail for tomorrow was in place.

Oh, she was tired, and there was still so much to be done.

Gabi headed to the ballroom to check on the setup.

'There are some more changes to be made to the

seating,' Bernadetta said by way of greeting. 'The ex-wife doesn't want to be near the aunt...'

Gabi sighed; she had been working on the seating into the small hours of last night and the bride constantly rang in her changes.

'I'll leave you to take it from here,' Bernadetta told Gabi. She didn't even pretend now to be sick, or to be meeting with a client. She simply waltzed off and left it all to Gabi.

It was late Friday afternoon and most people were just finishing up for the weekend yet Gabi's work had barely begun. Bernadetta would appear tomorrow, around eleven, just as the guests started to arrive.

One benefit of Bernadetta being gone, though, was that she could take off her shoes, which Gabi did; the high heels were not ideal and after a day of wearing them her back was starting to ache.

This weekend would be, Gabi was sure, her last real chance to tell Alim she was pregnant before the baby was born. Matrimoni di Bernadetta did not have another wedding at the Lucia for three months. She would have had her baby by then and the Grande Lucia could well be sold.

Gabi honestly did not know what to do.

His power scared her and, if she was honest, Alim's cruel dismissal still angered her; furthermore, he had made it very clear that he did not want any consequence from that night.

A kick beneath her ribs made Gabi smile.

As tiny as her baby was, it certainly made itself known.

At her ultrasound, Gabi had chosen not to find out what she was having. Not because she wasn't curious, more she did not want the baby's sex to have any bearing on the conversation, if she told Alim.

If she told him.

She was still troubled and unsure as to what to do.

Gabi stood in the ballroom and looked at the shower of stars that the chandelier created and recalled the bliss of dancing right here, alone with Alim, and how deeply happy she had been that night.

It brought her such pleasure to recall it.

The photographer had not forgotten and indeed the image of the two of them that night now lived on her tablet. It had been her screensaver for a while but that had proved too painful, so she had taken it down and now Gabi barely looked at it.

It had always hurt too much to do so, but time perhaps *was* kind, because Gabi hadn't really been able to recall, with clarity, the bliss of them together.

Until now.

But on this afternoon, with her baby wriggling inside her, she remembered how the shadows of the branches outside had crept across the walls, how Alim had, without a word, asked her to dance.

Yes, Gabi was a dreamer, but it was a memory that she was lost in now.

And that was how he found her.

It had been a busy day for Alim.

And a hellish few months.

His sister Yasmin had created her own share of

scandal at the wedding all those months ago, and Alim had been trying his best to sort that out.

Also, he had known the moment that diktat had been invoked that it would be impossible to be around Gabi and not want her. He took the laws of his land seriously. Now he walked into the ballroom with the first of the potential buyers and there was Gabi, holding her shoes and gazing up.

It was safer, far safer that she be gone.

'Is everything okay, Gabi?' Alim asked her, and his words were a touch stern.

'Oh!'

She turned and for the first time since that morning she saw him.

He was wearing a dark navy suit and looked stunning as usual; she had never felt more drab, standing barefoot in an ill-fitting suit.

He was with a man she recognised as Raul Di Savo.

Gabi pushed out a smile and tried to be polite but her heart was hammering.

'Yes, everything is fine. I was just trying to work out the table plan for Saturday.'

'We have a large wedding coming up,' Alim explained to Raul.

'And both sets of parents are twice divorced.' Gabi gave a slight eye-roll, and then chatted away as she bent to put on her shoes, trying to keep things about work. 'Trying to work out where everyone should be seated is proving—'

'Gabi!' Alim scolded, and then turned to Raul.

'Gabi is not on my staff. *They* tend to be rather more discreet.' He waved his hand in dismissal. 'Excuse us, please.'

Just like that he dismissed her.

He knew that he had hurt her, for that morning she had left there had been so much promise between them and now she looked at him with funeral eyes. Alim could see the pain and bewildered confusion there.

He wanted to wave his hand to Raul and tell him to get the hell out of the ballroom. He wanted to take her to bed.

She did not leave quietly.

Gabi slammed the door on her way out and Alim and Raul stood in the ballroom with the lights dancing in the late afternoon sun.

'What is the real reason you are selling?' Raul asked him.

Raul knew the business was thriving and he wanted to know why Alim was letting it go. And Raul knew too that Alim could so easily outsource the management of the hotel as he moved his portfolio back to the Middle East.

Alim had brought him here to give the true answer, and now he tried to drag his mind back to the sale, yet Gabi's fragrance hung in the air, along with the memory of their dance.

'When I bought the hotel those had not been cleaned in years,' Alim said, gesturing to the magnificent lights and remembering when the moon had lit them. 'Now they are taken down regularly and cared for properly. It is a huge undertaking. The room has to be closed so no functions can be held, and it is all too easy to put it off.'

'I leave all that to my managers to organise,' Raul said.

Alim nodded. 'Usually I do too, but when I took over the Grande Lucia there had been many cost-cutting measures. It was slowly turning into just another hotel. It is not just the lighting in the ballroom, of course. What I am trying to explain is that this hotel has become more than an investment to me. Once I return to my homeland I shall not be able to give it the attention it deserves.'

'The next owner might not either,' Raul pointed out.

'That is his business. But while the hotel is mine I want no part in her demise.'

'Now you have given me pause for thought,' Raul admitted.

'Good.' Alim smiled. 'The Grande Lucia deserves the best caretaker. Please,' Alim said, indicating that their long day of meetings had come to an end, for he needed badly to be alone, 'take all the time you need to look around and to enjoy the rest of your stay.'

Alim walked out of the ballroom and he was conflicted.

So badly he wanted to seek her out. More worryingly, though, he wanted to work out a chance for them. The only place they could speak was the desert.

He could just imagine Gabi's reaction if he suggested that!

He was informed that Bastiano Conti, who had flown in from Sicily, had just arrived at the hotel. They were, in fact, friends, and would often hit the casinos and clubs together. Those carefree days were gone now, yet they were not the ones Alim craved.

It was one woman, and the hope for one more night with her that could be his undoing.

Alim went and greeted Bastiano and was grateful to hear that he had plans for tonight and would be entertaining guests.

'We will meet tomorrow?' Bastiano checked, and Alim was about to agree.

The hotel had to be sold after all and Raul seemed set to decline.

Yet Alim's problems were greater than real estate, and he watched his friend and potential buyer raise a surprised eyebrow as Alim, usually the consummate host, rearranged their plans.

'Bastiano, I deeply apologise, but I am going to have to reschedule the viewing. I have to return to my country tonight.'

There was not a hope of being in the same country, let alone the same building, as Gabi, and abiding by the rules.

His rapid departure from the Grande Lucia was unnecessary, though, because Gabi was no longer in the building.

By the time his private jet lifted into the sky, she was in the infirmary.

FREE Merchandise is 'in the Cards' for you!

Dear Reader,

We're giving away FREE MERCHANDISE!

Seriously, we'd like to reward you for reading this novel by giving you **FREE MERCHANDISE** worth over **$20** retail. And no purchase is necessary!

You see the Jack of Hearts sticker above? Paste that sticker in the box on the Free Merchandise Voucher inside. Return the Voucher today… and we'll send you Free Merchandise!

Thanks again for reading one of our novels—and enjoy your Free Merchandise with our compliments!

Pam Powers

Pam Powers

P.S. Look inside to see what Free Merchandise is **"in the cards"** for you!

W

e'd like to send you two free books like the one you are enjoying now. Your two books have a combined cover price of over $10 retail, but they are yours to keep absolutely FREE! We'll even send you 2 wonderful surprise gifts. You can't lose!

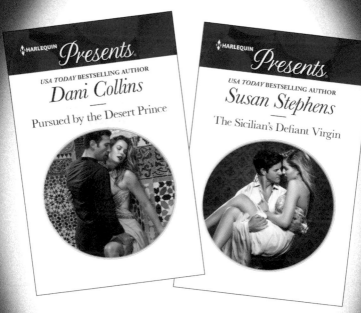

REMEMBER: Your Free Merchandise, consisting of **2 Free Books** and **2 Free Gifts**, is worth over $20 retail! No purchase is necessary, so please send for your Free Merchandise today.

Get TWO FREE GIFTS!

We'll also send you 2 wonderful FREE GIFTS (worth about $10 retail), in addition to your 2 Free books!

Visit us at:

www.ReaderService.com

Books received may not be as shown.

YOUR FREE MERCHANDISE INCLUDES...
2 FREE Books **AND** 2 FREE Mystery Gifts

FREE MERCHANDISE VOUCHER

2 FREE BOOKS and **2 FREE GIFTS**

Please send my Free Merchandise, consisting of
2 Free Books and **2 Free Mystery Gifts**.
I understand that I am under no obligation to buy
anything, as explained on the back of this card.

❏ I prefer the regular-print edition
106/306 HDL GLTH

❏ I prefer the larger-print edition
176/376 HDL GLTH

Please Print

FIRST NAME

LAST NAME

ADDRESS

APT.#   CITY

STATE/PROV.   ZIP/POSTAL CODE

NO PURCHASE NECESSARY!

P-517-FMIVY17

▲ Detach card and mail today. No stamp needed. ▲

® and ™ are trademarks owned and used by the trademark owner and/or its licensee.
© 2016 HARLEQUIN ENTERPRISES LIMITED. Printed in the U.S.A.

She had closed the ballroom door loudly on Alim, and at first had thought it was the shock of seeing him and being treated so coldly that had her doubling over.

It was then that her waters had broken.

The staff at the Grande Lucia were more than used to slight dramas unfolding and to handling them discreetly, though Anya was clearly shocked.

'You're pregnant?' she asked in surprise.

'Is there anyone I can call for you?' she continued as she ushered Gabi into a small room behind Reception.

'Not yet.'

Oh, she would have to let Bernadetta know but Gabi could not even think of her now.

And, yes, she would have to tell her mother, but Carmel's anger and resentment had hurt Gabi so much already.

She just wanted to be alone now.

They waited for the ambulance to arrive and as they did, need spoke for her as inadvertently she said his name.

'Alim…' Gabi gasped.

'Don't worry,' Anya reassured her, assuming that Gabi was upset that she might have created a problem for the smooth running of the hotel, especially when he was showing potential buyers around. 'No one saw what happened. Anyway, he has already left.'

'Left?'

'He flew back to his country a little while ago.

Do you want me to call Marianna and let her know what is going on?'

Gabi didn't answer.

She was just trying to take in the news that Alim had gone.

A part of her had hoped that having seen her again in the ballroom he might later seek her out.

It would appear not.

Alim could not make it any clearer that he had no interest in her.

The ambulance did not come to the main entrance, for that might be distressing or cause disruption to some of the guests.

Gabi left by the trade entrance, to bear the child of both the owner of the Grande Lucia and Sultan of Zethlehan.

'It's too soon,' she pleaded to the doctor at the hospital as she fought not to bear down, but time was no longer being kind.

Like endless waves submerging her, there was no pause, no time to catch her breath and calm her racing mind.

Alim.

She wanted his presence and to be held once again in his arms.

Yet she had chosen not to tell him, and whether it would have made a difference or not, this night she gave birth alone.

As she screamed, her mind flashed to Fleur, who had taken this lonely journey also.

And she would never be her, Gabi swore.

Her daughter was born a short while later.

She was delivered onto her stomach and, instead of being whisked away, her little girl was vigorous and Gabi was able to hold her to her chest and gaze down at her daughter.

Oh, she was beautiful, with silky black hair and dark eyes that were almond-shaped, like her father's.

'We have to take her now to the nursery,' the nurse informed Gabi, and it physically hurt to let her baby go.

Soon, though, her mother arrived and it was comforting to make up.

'You have me,' Carmel said.

'I know.'

It felt good to know that, and there were other things to be grateful for.

The baby was strong. So strong, the nurse told her when Gabi got in to see her, for she breathed with just a little oxygen for assistance.

'Do you have a name for her?' Gabi was asked.

Gabi had thought she was having a son; she had been so sure that history was about to repeat itself, and that, like Fleur, she would bear the Sultan's firstborn son.

But history had not repeated itself.

Still, she was absolutely beautiful, a little ray of light, and Gabi knew in that moment what to call her.

'Lucia.'

'That's such a pretty name,' the nurse said.

It was the place where love had been made.

Alim needed to know that he had a daughter, Gabi

was painfully aware of that. But not now, not when she was so emotional and drained. Gabi was scared of what she might agree to. When she was stronger, she would work out how on earth to tell him.

Her mother came into the nursery to see her granddaughter. It was close to midnight and Carmel had been running errands for Gabi—packing a case and also letting Bernadetta know that not only would her very efficient assistant wedding planner not be there tomorrow but that there had also been a lot left undone tonight.

'Bernadetta is not best pleased,' she told Gabi. 'She wants to know if you sorted out the table plan.'

'No,' Gabi said, and she got back to gazing at her daughter.

Bernadetta, for once, could sort it all out.

Lucia was Gabi's priority now.

And always would be.

Whatever the future held.

CHAPTER NINE

'THE CONTRACTS ARE *still* with Bastiano?' Alim frowned when Violetta gave him the news. 'This should all have been dealt with by now.'

Despite Alim's rapid departure, an offer on the Grande Lucia had been made and accepted, but nearly three months later the sale seemed to have stalled.

Alim needed the hotel gone!

He sat in his sumptuous office in the palace and tried to take care of business with a mind that was elsewhere.

Seeing Gabi again had proved to be his undoing.

Temptation beckoned more with each passing day but never more so than now.

A wedding was being held there this weekend and Matrimoni di Bernadetta was the company that had been hired for the event.

The itinerary was open on his computer and Alim scrolled through it, hoping for a glimpse of her name, or a note that she might have left in the margins, as Gabi often did.

There was none, though.

'Do you want me to contact his attorney?' Violetta asked, but Alim shook his head.

'I will speak with Bastiano myself,' Alim said.

He might even speak with him face to face.

Alim was sorely tempted to summon the royal jet, with the excuse of meeting with Bastiano, but really for the chance to see Gabi.

He was dangerously close to breaking the diktat.

'That will be all,' Alim said, and, having dismissed Violetta, he attempted to deal with the day's correspondence.

He didn't get very far.

It had been months since he had seen Gabi again but the feelings had not faded.

If anything, they had intensified for, despite the pressure his father and the elders exerted, Alim was no closer to agreeing to a wedding.

His mind was in Rome, rather than here in Zethlehan, where it should belong.

He thought of the days he had loved most at the Grande Lucia.

Gabi, arriving early in the morning, and how she would become increasingly frazzled throughout the working day.

And he thought too of the wedding nights, and how she would finally relax again and enjoy watching the show she had produced.

He missed her.

Not the risqué life he had once led, but the small moments that were now long gone—stepping through the brass doors and seeing her sitting in the lounge with Marianna. Knowing that there would be another wedding soon and the chance to see her again had brought him more pleasure than he had realised at the time.

His times at the hotel had been made better by her—the scent of flowers coming from the ballroom and Gabi directing brass trolleys laden with gifts and arrangements...

Alim missed those times.

And they would soon be gone for ever.

He had done all he could to sever his ties to Rome, yet it felt as if his heart had been left there.

He looked up as his mother knocked at his open office door and he shook his head.

'Not now,' Alim said.

'Yes, now,' Rina said and came in.

He had always been polite—if a little distant—with others, though now he was stone cold.

The vast palace felt too small, and there was no company that he wished to keep.

Unless it was Gabi's.

'How are you, Alim?'

Alim didn't even bother to lie and pretend that he was fine, he just gave a shrug. 'I am trying to chase up the contracts for the Grande Lucia. I think I might need to make a trip to Italy.'

'When?'

'Soon,' Alim said.

He would be courting temptation if he went back this weekend, Alim knew, yet he had to see Gabi.

'I have just held the morning meeting with your father. He thinks that a wedding would cheer Yasmin up.'

'I am not going to marry to provide a remedy for my sister's mood.'

'What about your mood, Alim?' Rina said. 'You are not happy.'

'No,' he admitted. 'But I do not need to be happy to do my work.' And there was indeed work to be done so he gestured for his mother to take a seat. 'Kaleb's thirtieth is coming up...'

But his mother was not here about that. 'I am concerned, Alim. I thought once you were home you might be happy, but it has been months now...'

'I love my land.'

'Yet you make no commitment to remain here?'

'You mean a bride?' Always the conversation led back to that. 'A bride is not the solution.'

'Then tell me the problem.'

'No.'

He did not share his thoughts, let alone his feelings, with others. In fact, until recently he had refused to examine them.

Life had always been about duty and work and solving problems logically.

Now, for the first time in his life, he could not come up with a solution to the dilemma he faced.

'Alim,' his mother implored. 'Speak to me.'

He did not know how to start.

'I might understand,' Rina insisted.

Yes, she just might, Alim thought, for there was no doubt that hers was a loveless marriage.

'Just before the diktat was invoked I met someone,' Alim said, but, even as he explained things, he
knew that wasn't quite right. 'I have liked her for a
couple of years but I always stayed back. Things got
more serious just before I was summoned home. I
left her without any real explanation and when I returned to Rome the other month…'

He didn't finish. Alim could not explain the sadness in Gabi's eyes, neither did he want to reveal the
ache in his heart and the regret for the year together
that had been denied them.

Alim knew it could never have been more than
a year; his father would never give his approval to
Gabi.

No, his bride would be from Zethlehan. In fact,
his father had whittled it down to the final three—
the one who would uphold tradition and best serve
the country, and was deeply schooled in their ways,
would be Oman's choice.

'I am thinking of going to Rome to see her.'

His mother was quiet for some considerable time
and when she spoke her voice was strained and laced
with fear. 'Have you broken the diktat, Alim?'

'No.'

He heard his mother breathe out in relief. 'That's
good, then.'

'How can it be good?'

All that mattered to them was that he abided by
the rules, no matter the cost to himself.

'There is a desert out there, Alim,' Rina said, and
he stood and looked out the window; the reproach

in his voice was aimed at himself, for of course he had considered it.

'Gabi will not be coming to the desert. She would never even entertain the thought.'

'She does not have to reside there,' Rina said. 'She could visit now and then and once you are married, once you have an heir...' It was a difficult conversation to have. 'Well, then the rules relax.'

And he threw his mother a look. 'Do you think I would do to my wife what my father did to you?'

The poorly kept secret was finally being discussed.

'I would never impose a loveless marriage on a bride,' Alim said, and then he closed his eyes because that was exactly what it would be, and the reason that, despite mounting pressure, still he refused marriage. 'I hate how you have been treated,' Alim told his mother.

He thought of them smiling on the palace balcony or waving and chatting as they arrived at a function.

Then the relative silence that would descend when they returned to their private lives—his mother would retreat to her wing, his father to his.

'Do I look unhappy, Alim?' Rina asked.

He looked over. No, her features were relaxed and, as she often did, Rina smiled her gentle smile.

'You barely communicate,' Alim pointed out, but his mother shook her head. 'I have just come from a meeting with your father—we have one each working day.'

Alim accepted that, but that was for the running

of the country—a private life between them did not exist. 'You sleep in a separate wing of the palace.'

'And we do so at my request,' Rina said. 'Alim, I love my country. Growing up, I always knew that I would likely be chosen and that I would one day be queen. I did my duty, I had three beautiful children who I have raised well; I continue to work hard for my country and I live a very privileged life.'

Rina knew she needed to say more.

Oh, she was very schooled in the rules, and had studied them closely.

Yes, Zethlehan was progressive in many ways, for *all* needs were served.

Save love, for it was not taken into consideration in the rules.

Still, it was a delicate topic and Rina took a moment to consider before she spoke on. 'Alim, just because I don't have a loving marriage, it does not mean that I don't know love.'

Distracted by his thoughts of Gabi, it took a moment for his mother's words to sink in and he looked up at her.

Was she telling him that she had a lover?

That the times her husband was away were not so lonely after all, that she had her own reasons for sleeping in a separate wing of the palace?

The silence between them was loaded but Rina gave a slight shake of her head. 'I am saying no more than that.'

It was as if every grain of desert sand had shifted

as his mother told him without detail that she was happy. That somehow their relationship had been made to work for them.

'Your father and I have made it work for everyone…' Then she saw Alim's jaw tighten and amended, 'I do feel sorry for James,' she admitted. 'He deserves more of his father.' It was the first time his name had been spoken within these walls. 'That should have been handled better, but it is your father who makes the rules.'

Alim nodded.

'Talk to your love, Alim.'

'I did not say anything about love.'

'Talk to your lover, then. That is the one solution to all ills.'

'How?' he asked. 'She would never come to the desert.'

'I have studied this very closely.' Rina smiled and tapped the hated large, leather-bound file that sat on his desk. 'There is nowhere in the diktat that mentions phones.'

Alim smiled.

'If anyone can sort things out, it is you.'

Alim was not so sure but he knew that neither distance nor silence was working.

And it was for that reason that he picked up the phone and, rather than chase up Bastiano regarding the sale, he called the reception desk at the Grande Lucia.

'*Pronto*. May I speak with Gabi?'

'Gabi?' The female voice that answered was an

unfamiliar one and didn't seem to know to whom Alim was referring.

'She is organising a wedding there,' he explained.

'Oh, that Gabi!' came the response, and it was clear that she now knew who Alim meant. 'I think she is still on maternity leave.'

'Maternity leave?'

The palace must be sitting on a fault line, Alim thought, because for the second time in an hour the sands seemed to shift.

'I think you have the wrong person,' he said, but the receptionist wasn't listening—she was talking to a colleague. Alim could hear his rapid breathing as in the background a male voice spoke and then the receptionist amended her words.

'No, no, my mistake.'

Alim didn't even have a chance to register relief before she spoke again.

'Apparently Gabi is back from her leave today.'

Alim's mind worked rapidly,

If indeed Gabi had been on maternity leave then the baby *had* to be his. It was practically nine months to the day since they had slept together and she had certainly been a virgin then.

Yet the dates confused him. Alim certainly wasn't an expert in pregnancy, but this woman was telling him that Gabi was already *back* from maternity leave.

Alim thought of the last time he had seen Gabi and she hadn't looked pregnant, but, then again, he had done all he could not to look at her.

Alim knew that he had to speak with Gabi.

Alone.

But how?

A possibility was starting to come to mind and when he spoke his voice was even and calm, for Alim rarely revealed his emotions.

'Actually, rather than Gabi, may I speak with Bernadetta?'

'Can I ask who is calling?'

'It is Alim.'

He heard her nervous gasp. 'Sultan al—'

Alim spoke over her, for his patience was running out. 'Just get Bernadetta on the line.'

He stood and, just as he had needed air the day his father had invoked the diktat, he walked out of the French windows and onto the large balcony.

Unlike then, the air was not cool, it was hot and dry, though it was calming to Alim and he gladly breathed it in, his eyes narrowing against the fierce sun as he looked out at the desert.

He could speak with Gabi there, unheard by others; only there could they discuss things fully.

There was no doubt a frantic search was under way at the Grande Lucia for the rather elusive Bernadetta and it gave time for Alim's plans to take better shape.

'Pronto,' he said when a nervous Bernadetta finally came to the phone.

'Sultan Alim…' Bernadetta attempted to purr into the phone but it was more of a croak. 'How lovely to hear from you. It's been a long time.'

'Indeed. I was wondering,' Alim said, 'if Matrimoni di Bernadetta had the necessary skills to co-organise a royal wedding here in Zethlehan.'

He heard her slight gasp. 'Of course. It would be not just an honour but a pleasure...' Bernadetta fawned but Alim swiftly broke in.

'Then I need Gabi here by tomorrow,'

'Gabi? Oh, no, I wouldn't be sending my assistant!' Bernadetta immediately responded. 'I would take care of every detail myself—'

'Bernadetta,' Alim interrupted her again. 'You have a good head for business and you hire only the best, but we both know that it is Gabi who turns a wedding into an unforgettable creation.'

He soothed her vast ego yet he got to the point.

'I want Gabi here.'

'Indeed, she's excellent, but Gabi might not be available to travel at short notice. You see, she has recently—'

Alim swiftly cut in. He did not want Bernadetta to reveal that Gabi had just had a baby. Alim was very well aware that should Gabi find out that he knew, there would not be a hope in hell of getting her to agree to come to Zethlehan.

Yet he wanted Gabi to tell him to his face.

'I don't care how busy she is with the current wedding. I do not care about her personal life and whether she has plans that she cannot change. If you want the contract for the wedding, then Gabi is to be here by tomorrow.'

Alim spoke like the Sultan he was and Bernadetta responded accordingly.

'And she shall be.'

Alim let out a breath and there followed a giddy sensation of relief that had nothing to do with what he had just discovered.

More that he would finally see Gabi.

She had been missed more than even Alim had wanted to admit.

'If, when you meet with Gabi,' Bernadetta said, 'you have any concerns...'

'I shan't be meeting with Gabi,' Alim said, anticipating Gabi's resistance to the suggestion that she come here. 'I am only making this initial contact. I don't want to be troubled with minor details. From now on, everything will be dealt with by the palace aide, Violetta.'

He gave Bernadetta a few more rapid details and then ended the call.

He looked out at the desert again and the golden sight soothed, for there solutions could more readily be found.

Alim walked back into his office, trying to take in that he could well be a father and trying to fathom all that Gabi would have been through.

He summoned Violetta.

She was more than used to dealing with scandal and had her work cut out for her in dealing with the al-Lehans.

And not just his father and James, Alim now knew, for it would seem that even his mother had a secret life of her own. One that Alim had had no clue about.

A baby.

He did not know if it was a boy or girl and Alim knew all the problems it could create.

Yet as he waited for Violetta to arrive, despite the news, his overriding feeling was relief.

Gabi would be here soon.

He looked up as Violetta came in and, without asking, she closed the door and came over to the desk.

'I require your discretion,' Alim said.

'You have it.'

Violetta, too, was brilliant at her job.

CHAPTER TEN

'GABI! GABI!'

Bernadetta was almost running through the foyer towards her.

Gabi was carrying a glass vase containing an array of Sahara roses to take up to the bridal suite.

Housekeeping should have already dealt with it but things at the Grande Lucia had got a little slack now that Alim wasn't around.

'Yes?' she answered wearily.

It was Gabi's first official day back at work and it felt as if she had never been away.

It had been hard leaving Lucia but her mother had promised to drop by with her at lunchtime so that Gabi could give her a cuddle.

Gabi could only hope there was time to actually take her lunch break!

There were so many boxes not ticked and a lot of things that should have long ago been taken care of which had been left for Gabi's return; she had just this minute come from a stand-up row with the very temperamental chef.

'I know this will come as a shock…' Bernadetta said, and Gabi stopped herself from rolling her eyes—there had been so many shocks this morning!

The cake had been confirmed for *next* Saturday, Gabi had found out.

The flowers had not, as Gabi had first thought, gone missing; instead, they had been delivered, as per Matrimoni di Bernadetta's instructions, to last week's wedding venue.

Chaos was all around.

The chef had not been informed that there were not only eighteen guests requiring the gluten-free option but that there were four vegans, two raw vegans, four kosher and five halal.

No, there was very little that might come as a shock, save that the groom had run off!

Gabi was about to be proved wrong.

'Matrimoni di Bernadetta has been invited to co-organise Sultan Alim's wedding…'

Gabi nearly dropped the vase.

What the hell was Alim thinking?

Or, more likely, he wasn't thinking, at least not about her.

His wedding needed to be organised and he had simply called on the best, without any consideration of the pain that it might cause her.

But then Bernadetta spoke on.

'Alim has asked that you fly there tomorrow and meet with his assistant.'

This time Gabi did drop the vase, for there was no one crueller in that moment than Alim.

It shattered loudly as it hit the floor and the water and crystal was strewn along with the gorgeous roses.

Gabi barely looked down and neither did Bernadetta.

'I can't,' Gabi said. 'It's impossible. I have a new baby…'

'I know that,' Bernadetta said.

'I can't leave her.' And then fear clutched at her heart because maybe Alim knew. Maybe he was planning for her to bring the baby… 'Lucia hasn't had all her inoculations.'

'Oh, for God's sake,' Bernadetta snorted. 'Do you really think I'd send you with a baby on such an important job?'

'Did you tell Alim about her?' Gabi was on her knees and trying not to cry as she scrabbled to pick up the crystal, her mind racing in fear as she thought of Alim plotting to whisk Lucia away.

Yes, Gabi was a dreamer, and some of them were nightmares.

'Of course I didn't tell the Sultan. Why would he care? This is a royal wedding he's asking us to organise.' Bernadetta was nearly shouting. 'He doesn't want to hear about your personal life.'

'I don't want to go,' Gabi said. 'Send someone else.'

'Alim wants you, though. He says you have an eye for attention and…' Bernadetta almost choked on her next words. 'He told me that he wants you adequately remunerated…' And then she told her the figure that Alim was offering just for this short trip.

Was this his way of apologising? Gabi wondered. Was this Alim's strange way of making amends?

As Sophie came over to help clear up the mess that had been made, Gabi sank back on her heels for a second and tried to make sense of things, not that Bernadetta gave her a moment to gather her thoughts.

'Gabi, if you cost me this contract, don't even bother turning up for work again. And don't think I shan't tell everyone that you were the one who blew the deal.'

Bernadetta stalked off and Gabi just sat there.

'I can mop around you.' Sophie smiled and then she helped Gabi up.

'I don't want to leave my baby.'

'Then don't go,' Sophie said. 'Tell her to get lost.'

And Gabi smiled because Sophie was Sicilian and rather feistier than she, but then Gabi's smile wavered and tears were dangerously close. 'I don't want to organise his wedding.'

She had said too much, Gabi knew, but Sophie was her dear, dear friend, though even she did not guess that Alim was Lucia's father.

'Did you have a crush on him?' Sophie asked.

Yes, he was as unattainable to the likes of Gabi as that.

Her mother, when she brought in Lucia, wasn't exactly gushing with excitement at the prospect of her daughter flying off to the Middle East.

They met in the foyer and there was only time

for a very brief cuddle with Lucia as she told her mother the news.

'Gabi, isn't it time you looked for a more practical job?'

'I love my work,' Gabi said. 'I'm good at what I do.'

'Of course, but some dreams you have to let go of when you have a baby. When I found out I was pregnant with you I had to give up my studies...'

Gabi closed her eyes, she had heard it all many times before.

Only history wasn't repeating itself.

She held Lucia to her cheek and breathed in the soft baby scent.

If anything, Lucia made her want to achieve more; her love for her daughter drove Gabi to be better rather than less. And, yes, it would be hard to leave her, but the money would certainly help, as well as the boost to her career.

But more than that, so much more than that, she would be able to tell Lucia her history for she would have seen Alim's country first hand.

Gabi had grown up not knowing anything about her father; her daughter would not suffer the same fate.

'Are you able to look after Lucia for two nights?'

'You know I shall.'

Gabi thanked her mother. She knew Lucia would be beautifully taken care of, and though it was her first concern it wasn't the only one—Gabi wanted to be very sure she wasn't walking into a trap.

So, to be sure, she called the number she had been given by Bernadetta.

Violetta's voice was familiar and Gabi recalled that she had dealt with the hotel arrangements for Marianna when Mona and James had married.

Now Gabi knew why.

'Alim is concerned that his European guests will not understand Zethlehan ways,' Violetta explained. 'He said that you have a good eye for detail. We want the wedding to be seamless and all the guests' needs attended to.'

'Who shall I be liaising with?'

'Mainly me, but also the hotel manager at the venue where the commoner guests shall be housed. That is where you shall be staying during this visit, so you can work from a visual.'

'I see.'

There was no firm date yet but Violetta ran through the guest list. Some of the names were familiar. Bastiano Conti was amongst them and Gabi knew he was not just a friend of Alim's but about to be the new owner of the Grande Lucia.

It sounded legit.

Yes, it was more lavish and complex than anything she had dealt with before but, at the end of the day, it sounded like just another wedding to plan.

And so for now she dealt with it as such.

'Where will the service be held?'

'There will be two services,' Violetta explained. 'A small, very intimate gathering of family and elders, but we would take care of that. Following the formal service there will be a large reception back at the palace. We need you to help transport the guests and to ensure that they wear suitable attire.' She went through the dress codes with Gabi. 'Also, all dietary requirements from them must come through you.'

Yes, just like any other wedding!

'When you are here,' Violetta continued, 'you can speak with the palace head chef, so it might be helpful if you could bring some menu suggestions that he can incorporate. The banquet will be traditional but we want alternatives that can cater to all palates.'

'I see.' Gabi swallowed and forced herself to delve a little deeper. 'When I get there and speak to Sultan Alim I can ask him—'

'Oh, no,' Violetta quickly broke in. 'While I understand that you worked alongside the Sultan at the Grande Lucia, things are very different here. You will not have access to the Sultan; you will deal directly with me.'

And that was the real reason she agreed.

Gabi needed contacts, and not of the usual kind, and Violetta would be a very good one to have. One day she would be ready to tell Alim about Lucia and, as she was fast finding out, you didn't just call up a palace and ask to be put through to the Sultan.

And so, to Bernadetta's delight, Gabi said yes.

'You need to go home and prepare.' Bernadetta, for the first time ever, insisted that Gabi leave early. 'You have black trousers…?' she checked.

Gabi's curves had returned and she felt Bernadetta's disapproval as she looked over her figure.

'I do.'

She just hoped they would fit.

'What about this wedding?' Gabi asked Berna-detta. 'There's still so much to be done.'

'I think I can manage,' Bernadetta said, 'though if you could sort out the flowers before you go…'

Lazy to the last, Gabi thought.

Sophie found her a new vase and Gabi's hands were shaking as she rearranged the flowers. She heard an email ping in.

Gabi saw that it was from Violetta and picked up her tablet to read it. She would fly tomorrow at mid-day and the flight was first class.

It was all a little overwhelming.

Not the itinerary and not just leaving little Lucia but that the man she loved was getting married.

How? Gabi thought as she walked out of the office with the flowers. She did not know *how* her heart could still beat while planning his wedding.

'Hey.'

A man called out to her as she went to take the roses up to the bridal suite and, distracted, she nodded at the handsome stranger.

'Gabi!'

He called out her name.

'Oh!' She stopped when she realised that it was Raul, one of the potential buyers for the hotel, and then she remembered how he would know her. 'You were in the ballroom when Alim…' Her voice trailed off as she recalled how Alim had scolded and then dismissed her that day.

It had been the day Lucia had been born!

Oh, she had been cross, so cross with Alim, though this stranger was clearly not to blame for that!

'I'm hoping to meet with Alim.'

'Good luck!' Gabi rolled her eyes. 'He's back home.'

'Oh!'

'For his wedding.'

'I see.'

'I'm planning it, actually.'

She felt as if she was about to cry.

'Can you let him know I need to speak with him?'

'I'm a wedding planner,' Gabi said, and she let a little of her anger out before walking off. 'I don't get access to the Sultan.'

Saying goodbye to Lucia was incredibly hard.

She had already been staying at her mother's this weekend.

Going back to work yesterday and leaving little Lucia for twelve hours had seemed agony at the time but now she would be away for two days and two nights.

One day would be spent travelling to Zethlehan, then a night at a luxurious hotel followed by a day of meetings with Violetta.

The second night would be spent travelling back to Rome and then finally she would see Lucia again.

Gabi had been unable to feed Lucia herself, so there wasn't any problem with that, but it ached to see her little girl asleep in her crib and to know that she was about to leave.

'Don't wake her,' Carmel said, because she could see that Gabi was about to pick her up.

'I'm going to miss her.'

'Gabi, even if you weren't going to Zethlehan you would barely have seen her this weekend, what with the wedding and everything.'

'I know.'

Her hours were proving difficult and Gabi knew she was asking a lot from her mother just to keep her job. Carmel had raised one child alone and did not want to do it again. Right now, there were bills that needed to paid and so Carmel had agreed to help with Lucia for a few months, but after that…

'You could work with Rosa,' Carmel said.

Gabi had considered it, yet, as much as she cared for Rosa, Gabi did not want another boss. Still, it was the more practical solution and right now Gabi was beyond exhausted and could feel her grip loosening on her dreams.

Carmel went down to check if the taxi had arrived and Gabi kissed Lucia's little cheek and whispered that she was the sunshine of her life—*'Sei il sole della mia vita.'*

She wanted better for her, Gabi knew—which was part of the reason she was on her way to a new adventure.

What an adventure!

Gabi had flown before, but only within Italy and only for work.

Bernadetta, of course, would fly business class while Gabi sat way back in the bowels of the plane.

It was very different today!

Champagne was offered before they had even taken off but Gabi declined and took water as she was trying to be good. While the weight had fallen off while she'd been pregnant, Gabi had been thin for about two days after Lucia had been born and then her milk had come in, closely followed by the return of her curves.

A meal was served, then her bed prepared, while Gabi went and put on the pyjamas they offered her.

'Would you like to be woken for a meal before landing?'

It was a nine-hour flight to Zethlehan and Gabi was about to say that there was no chance of her *not* being woken, when again she was reminded that she was without Lucia.

'That would be lovely,' Gabi said.

The cabin lights were dimmed and Gabi lay there, sure, quite sure, that she would be too nervous to sleep.

Instead, she woke to a gentle shake of her shoulder and was informed that her meal would be served shortly; she had slept for seven hours. It wasn't just her first decent sleep since Lucia had been born, it was her first decent sleep since the morning Alim had so cruelly ended things.

Far from nervous, it was so nice to feel rested.

She made her way to the very nice bathroom where there was actually a shower. It felt wonderful to shower high in the sky and after she had washed and brushed her teeth and styled her hair, she took her Pill. Not that she would be needing it, but Gabi now took it every day. Not for this moment, and not to be ready for Alim, more because the absolute abandon between them that night had scared her.

In the cold light of day, she had realised that in bed with Alim she did not know her own mind.

In the deep of the night he had owned her so completely.

The absolute lack of thought and control had had her vow never to be so foolish again. No more chances.

Then she put on the heavy dark trouser suit and swore that if she ever did get her own business there would be a fitting, international choice.

Gabi returned to her seat and light refreshments and as she looked out over the ocean, Gabi amended that thought.

When she had her own business.

Sleep really was an amazing healer, and the distance from home combined with the white noise of the plane allowed her to think more clearly.

Alim had been harsh that morning when they had spoken and he had said that her mother used Gabi as an excuse. Yet he wasn't necessarily wrong.

Gabi didn't dwell on her mother's choices. She focussed instead on her own future, and her daughter's, for it was Lucia's future she wanted to improve upon too.

But first she had these days to get through.

Would she see him?

Gabi hoped so.

All the hurt, all the anger and the fact he was to marry should be enough to bury for good her feelings for him.

Yet they rose again and again, and more so since Lucia had been born, for every time she opened her eyes Gabi was reminded of the magic of him.

And the impossibility of them.

There were cross-winds, the pilot had warned them, and Gabi felt them as the plane came into land.

Her stomach lurched as she caught her first glimpse of the palace and it warned her of the might and power of the al-Lehan family.

It rose from a cliff edge, white and magnificent and looking out towards both ocean and city. And Zethlehan too was unexpected when seen from the air, for there was an eclectic mix of gleaming modern buildings that melded in with the old.

She had read up on the country's history and the royal family's lineage that went as far back as when the country had first been named.

It was progressive in many ways—a firstborn daughter could—and had—ruled this stunning land. The desert princess's husband and children had taken the al-Lehan name. And while there were some mentions of children borne from the harem, the rulings were clear—they were not considered part of the al-Lehan dynasty.

Children like Lucia and James were simply sidelined. They were shadow families, hidden away and never formally recorded or mentioned. Lucia deserved better. So did Gabi.

And she must never lose sight of that, Gabi thought as the wheels hit the runway.

She had arrived in Zethlehan, where the time, she was informed, was five p.m.

Remembering Violetta's instructions, Gabi put a scarf she had brought over her head and shoulders but it didn't fall as nicely, or as effortlessly, as the other women's, who made it look so easy.

She opened her tablet and the first thing she saw was a message from her mother with the most gorgeous picture of Lucia attached.

She was lying on her stomach and lifting her head up and smiling widely. Oh, it was surely Gabi's favourite photo and she touched the screen and traced her daughter's beautiful smile.

Gabi was wearing heels, on Bernadetta's instructions, and felt a head above all the delicate beauties as she disembarked. A wall of heat hit her as soon as she stepped off the plane. The wind was hot on her cheeks and the air burned as she breathed it in, but soon she was in the cool of the airport and she made a quick call home.

'Lucia is fine,' Carmel told her. 'Did you get the picture that I sent?'

'I did.' Gabi smiled.

'The reception is terrible,' Carmel said. 'I can hardly hear you.'

'I'll call again tomorrow,' Gabi told her mother. 'Give Lucia a kiss for me.'

Customs was straightforward as she had a letter of introduction from the palace and, given she had travelled only with hand luggage, in no time she was walking through to the arrivals lounge.

'Gabi!'

She recognised Violetta immediately and though they had only worked together briefly it was nice to see a familiar friendly face.

'How was your journey?' Violetta asked.

'It was wonderful,' Gabi said. 'I slept most of the way.'

'Good.' Violetta nodded. 'It is good that you are well rested. We are heading this way,' she explained. 'We are taking a helicopter.'

'A helicopter?' Gabi checked.

'Of course.'

Violetta said it so casually and Gabi assumed that when you worked with royalty then taking a helicopter must be to Violetta the equivalent of taking a taxi.

The chopper was waiting and Gabi climbed in and fastened her seat belt and put on the headphones that Violetta handed to her.

'It's very windy,' she warned Gabi. 'We might be in for a bit of a bumpy ride.'

Gabi felt her stomach curl as she was lifted high into the sky.

The airport was a little way out from the city and Gabi looked again at the amazing skyline that she had so recently seen from the plane.

The view was even more stunning than before. The sun was starting to set and the sky was such a blush pink that even the white palace in the distance seemed to have been painted rose. There was a haze over the city but then the helicopter banked to the right and she lost sight of it. Gabi craned her neck for a glimpse of the ocean to orientate herself but the view had disappeared from her window and so she turned her head to look for it on the other side.

It was way in the distance and Gabi felt her nostrils tighten as the palace faded from view.

Gabi looked over at Violetta, who was herself looking out of the window seemingly without concern.

Except even the city skyline had now faded and looking below there was only the occasional old building. 'Where are we going?' she asked Violetta.

There was no response.

Perhaps there were two cities, two palaces, Gabi told herself, while knowing that could not be right. Or maybe the pilot was diverting because of the wind?

Gabi had felt on high alert from the moment that she had agreed to come to Zethlehan but now she had her first taste of pure fear.

'Violetta,' Gabi said, more loudly this time.

Perhaps her microphone wasn't working, because Violetta did not respond to Gabi calling her name.

Now, as she looked out, there was nothing but desert. The sun was low in a burning sky and the endless sand looked like molten gold.

The ride seemed to take for ever, but finally coming into view she could see the billowing white of a desert abode.

* * *

And still Gabi fought for calm as she and Violetta disembarked.

What the hell had Bernadetta been thinking, making her wear heels? Gabi thought as she took off her shoes and then ran beneath the rotors.

'Is the service to be held in the desert?' Gabi asked, still fighting for an ordered reason, still hoping there was a sensible reason to explain why she had been brought here, but her voice was drowned by the rotors. 'Violetta?' she asked, and turned to see that Violetta was not by her side. She had run back under the rotors and was getting back into the chopper.

'Wait…' Gabi shouted.

Violetta did not.

The helicopter lifted into the blazing sky. The sand was a stinging blizzard of tiny, sharp pellets, and Gabi held her arms over her face to shield her eyes, eventually using her jacket to cover her nose and mouth. The soles of her feet were burning.

She had never felt more scared or alone, or more foolish for believing that she had been brought here for work.

And finally, when the helicopter was out of sight and the sands had somewhat settled she stood, windswept and scared but not alone.

There was Alim.

Only it was an Alim that Gabi had never seen.

Always he had been clean shaven, but not now.

Instead of the more familiar suits she was used

to seeing him in, Alim wore a black robe and on his head was a *keffiyeh*; he stood utterly still, imposing and straight, and Gabi felt as if she were his prey.

She remembered his father walking through the foyer and that moment of foreboding as she'd glimpsed the al-Lehans' power, and she felt the absolute full force of it now.

Yes, his prey was exactly what she was—he had sought her, found her and now she was within his grasp. As she stood there, waiting, they were plunged into darkness, for it was as if the desert had swallowed the fierce sun whole.

Gabi ran.

It was a rather stupid thing to do in a darkening desert but for now it didn't matter, she simply wanted to be away from him, only Gabi didn't get very far.

Alim caught up with her easily but so panicked was Gabi she shook off his hand from her arm and attempted to take off again, but she fell to the ground and lay with her head on her arm facing down, knowing that he stood over her.

Knowing there was nowhere to run.

'Gabi.'

His voice was annoyingly calm and terribly, achingly familiar.

Despite his attire, despite the unfamiliar surroundings, he was still the Alim she knew.

Gabi felt soothed when she should not, yet she could taste her panicked tears and feel the conflict for she wanted to turn around.

She wanted again to lift her face to him.

But anger won.

'You set me up,' she shouted, and thumped the ground.

'Come inside.'

'I don't want to come inside!'

Yet when he held out his hand she took it and she stood brushing herself down as the wind whipped her hair into her damp face.

So much for a sophisticated reunion!

'This is kidnap!'

'You are too dramatic.' Alim shrugged.

'Not where I come from. Your assistant told me I would not even have to see you...'

'Violetta ensured discretion,' Alim defended her. 'Don't you want a chance to be together for a while? I know that I do.' He had to shout to make himself heard over the wind. 'Don't you want a chance to speak and to catch up on all that has been going on?'

That was the very last thing that Gabi wanted!

Alim must not find out about Lucia while she was effectively stranded here.

'Come inside,' Alim said again, and the authoritarian note to his voice told her that he would not be argued with.

That did not stop Gabi. 'I don't want to.'

She shouted it but the wind whipped the words straight from her mouth and carried them into the night. Her mouth filled with sand and it was the most pointless argument ever, she knew, for she could not survive out here in this savage land.

Gabi had seen from the sky just how isolated they were.

He offered his hand to walk her back to the tent but Gabi declined it and for a few moments she stood her ground.

Alim would not stand in the fierce winds, attempting to persuade her. If she ran again he would find her in a matter of moments, for Alim knew the desert well and in her cumbersome clothes and winds such as these, Gabi would only manage a few steps.

Still, he was relieved to make it to the entrance and then turn around and sight her.

He waited, and after a short stand-off he could see that Gabi knew she was beaten.

There wasn't really a choice but to go inside and be with Alim.

The desert gave few options, she told herself.

The truth?

Gabi wanted to be with him.

CHAPTER ELEVEN

GABI WAS RELUCTANT to enter.

But for reasons of her own: she was scared she might like it.

Alim stood aside and Gabi stepped into relative silence.

She put down the shoes she carried in her hand, along with the small overnight bag, and felt him walk up behind her.

Her bare feet were caressed by soft rugs; oil lamps gave off a gentle glow that danced along the walls, though bore testimony to the fierce winds outside.

It was a haven indeed.

And she fought to keep her guard raised.

The peregrine note she had first breathed in when they'd danced was more prominent for Gabi now; it hung in the air and enveloped her from all around. It was hard to be scared with Alim so close by her side.

Gabi *was* angry, though.

'There is no one else here,' Alim informed her as he watched her walk through to the main living area.

She looked up at the high ceiling and felt terribly small. 'So there's no point screaming.'

Alim merely sighed. 'Gabi, you really are far too dramatic. What I meant when I said that we are alone is that there is no one here to disturb us and no one to overhear us when we are talking.'

He wanted to make it very clear to Gabi that whatever was said was just between them.

For now.

A baby certainly would change things—Violetta would have even more work cut out for her but at the very least he hoped by the end of this trip Gabi would leave knowing that both she and the baby would be taken care of.

Since he had found out that Gabi had been on maternity leave, Alim had been trying to find out what he could and using his best contacts to garner information.

It had proven surprisingly difficult.

Gabi did not work for the Grande Lucia; however, he had found out that indeed she had been on maternity leave. There was some recent CCTV footage of Gabi in the foyer of the Grande Lucia, speaking with a woman who handed Gabi a baby.

Alim had watched the grainy footage and had found himself holding his breath and zooming in on the image, desperate for a better glimpse of his child.

His child!

A fierce surge of protectiveness had hit him and his plans to bring Gabi to the desert had increased in their urgency.

He still did not know whether it was a boy or a girl.

And, from her silence, Alim was starting to realise that Gabi was in no rush to enlighten him with the news.

'I think,' Alim said, 'there is rather a lot to discuss, don't you?' But Gabi shook her head when he offered an opening for her to tell him.

'I have nothing to say to you.'

He was about to state that that was certainly not the case, but for now Alim chose to bide his time.

She was shocked, he accepted that, and angry too, so he offered her the chance to regroup.

'Why don't you go and get changed?' Alim suggested, and gestured to a curtained area.

'Changed?'

'Have a bath and get changed and then we can speak.'

'Alim, I'm stranded in the desert against my will and you expect me to go and slip into something more comfortable.'

'I don't like that suit.' Alim shrugged. 'And from memory neither do you.'

She just stood there.

The truth was, Gabi didn't really have anything more comfortable to put on.

Well, some pyjamas and another awful black suit and a small tube skirt and top.

Her packing really had been done in haste.

'My suits are all I've really got with me,' she admitted.

'I'm sure there will be alternatives in there.'

Again he gestured to the curtained area but still she did not move.

'Gabi, you are not stranded. If you want me to arrange the helicopter I shall do so, you just have to say the word.'

Gabi didn't, though.

She turned and walked to the area that Alim had gestured to and pulled aside heavy drapes.

It was like stepping inside a giant jewellery box.

The walls were lined with thick red velvet, which she ran her hand over, and jewelled lights dotted the ceiling.

It was a trove of exotic treasures with a huge, beautifully dressed bed in the centre.

She walked over and upon it lay a dark robe. It was too dark to make out the colour but the fabric when she held it was as soft as the velvet walls.

There was more—a dressing table adorned with stoppered bottles. Gabi picked up one and inhaled the musky fragrance then caught sight of herself in a large gilded mirror.

She looked terrible. Her hair was wild and filled with sand and the mascara she had put on in the bathroom of the plane was halfway down her cheeks.

Gabi looked over to a screened area and curiosity beckoned her to investigate.

The lighting was subtle and it was even darker behind the screen, but she could see a deep bath and it had been filled most of the way. Gabi put in her hand, assuming that the water would be cold.

Yet it was not.

Her fingers lingered, feeling the oily warmth for a moment, and she simply didn't understand so she walked back out to Alim.

He was lying on some cushions, propped up on one elbow and completely unfazed by her rather angry approach.

'You said that there was no one else here.'

'There isn't.'

'So who filled my bath?'

He looked over to where she stood and smiled at the suspicion in her eyes and then the slight startle in them when he gave his response.

'Me.'

'You?'

'The water comes directly from hot desert springs and I added some oils that are supposed to aid in relaxation.'

A slight shiver went through her, albeit a pleasurable one, as she thought of Alim here alone and readying the place for her arrival. But Gabi was in no mood to relax.

She wanted her wits about her, and knew that she needed to keep every one of them firing in his presence.

'Did you select the robe?' Gabi asked with a slight edge to her voice.

'No,' Alim responded. 'That would be Violetta.'

'So she lays out the clothes for your tarts?'

'Violetta has worked hard to ensure we are both comfortable and alone. We shall dine when you are ready to.'

'I ate on the plane.'

'Then there's no rush. Take your time.'

Gabi hadn't heard those words in a very long time; there simply weren't enough minutes in any day to get all she wanted to done.

Taking her time to get changed for dinner sounded like a reward on its own.

She wanted, for argument's sake, to say something scathing, but there was nothing that came to mind. Gabi wanted to point out that she was here against her wishes.

Yet her wishes said otherwise, for the truth was that she wanted to be there.

'Gabi.' He tried to capture her gaze but she would not let him. 'There is unfinished business between us.'

'I don't know what you mean.'

'Are you saying that you haven't thought of me?' Alim asked.

'I've tried everything I can not to.'

'Did it work?'

No.

Her silence said it for her, but then came the surprise when Alim spoke.

'It didn't work for me either.'

Her eyes flicked to his and she saw the burn of desire there, and while she was angry it was tempered with relief. Absolute relief, not just at seeing him but that clearly Alim had wanted to see her again too.

Gabi had ached not only because of the sudden end to their affair but its lack of closure.

There was so much unanswered.

She'd felt as if she had been slowly going out of her mind these past months.

Not just about the pregnancy but over and over she had relived their night together, and the morning after, like a perpetual film that restarted the moment it was over, pausing, analysing and trying to work out where it had all gone wrong.

And she wanted to know.

'Go,' Alim said.

He watched her turn and disappear and he was glad of it, for there was such dark temptation between them and that did not make for sensible conversation.

In their months apart he had told himself that possibly he looked back at their time through rose-coloured glasses and that abstinence had made his memory of her grow fonder.

Not so.

And consequently he dismissed her.

She turned, and as the drape swished closed behind her it became a boudoir indeed, Gabi thought as she returned to the dimly lit cavern.

She took off her suit and top and then her underwear and there was no feeling of being rushed or concern that she might be disturbed.

Oh, there were no locks or doors but this space was so deeply feminine she just knew it had been assigned to her.

Assigned.

Gabi stepped into the bath. She did not like that word, though she knew that it was the correct one.

This mini desert kingdom was a lover's hideaway.

But she would not be his lover tonight.

Her anger at being brought here against her will served only to inflame her temper, and her blood was surely a full degree warmer as she could feel its warm passage through her veins and the weight and heat in her breasts and groin.

She wrenched herself from the bath but there were no towels or sheets to drape herself in and Gabi was certainly not going to ask him for one. And she did not put on the oils left out for her, or the rouge for her lips or kohl.

Instead, she ran a silver comb through her hair and still dripping wet she pulled on the robe over her naked body. It was a deep purple and the scooped neckline showed too much cleavage while the velvet clung to her skin. She could deny to herself her desire for Alim, but the reflection in the mirror stated otherwise.

Her eyes were glittering, her cheeks were flushed and it looked as if she had just come.

Or was about to.

Alim was sitting at a low table and watched as Gabi walked out.

The gown clung becomingly to her skin, her hair fell in one long damp coil and was twisted so that it fell over her right shoulder and dripped onto her breast.

'Oh, you didn't have to go to all this effort,' she

teased as she took a seat opposite, assuming Violetta had prepared the treats and she simply hadn't noticed until now.

'Why wouldn't I?'

'I meant,' Gabi said, her voice a touch shrill, 'that clearly Violetta has been busy.'

'I selected the banquet,' Alim said. He picked up a jewelled flask and poured a clear-looking fluid into her glass. As he did so, a citrus scent coiled up in the air. 'And Violetta ensured it was all prepared, as best as it could be. However, while you were bathing I took care of the last-minute details.'

Her eye roll told her she did not believe him for a moment.

'You don't seem to understand the privacy afforded us here,' Alim said as he offered her delicacies. 'A woman is not brought here to work.'

Gabi peeled open the pastry she had selected; it was plump with succulent meat and ripe, pink pomegranate seeds. Gabi understood his words but she would not succumb to seduction. 'Why? Because you don't want her to be too tired for sex?'

He smiled that slow smile and she forgot his might, for he was Alim and they could just as easily be in the Grande Lucia, smiling across the foyer.

'Or too tired for conversation,' Alim said. 'Or too tired to lie on a clear night and look at the stars. There are many reasons other than sex to come deep into the desert. Let's explore them, shall we?'

And Gabi breathed out for he had done it again—

just as she'd thought she had scored a point he trumped her.

Sex was the uncomplicated part.

'It has been a long time since we have spoken,' Alim said, inviting conversation.

'I don't think there's anything to discuss.' She gave him a smile then, but it was far from sweet. 'Apart from the reason I'm here—your wedding!' And then the bitter smile faded and for a moment she came close to crumbling and she revealed a little of her pain. 'How cruel you are!'

'Gabi, you are not here to plan my wedding. I invented that, just so that we could be alone.'

'Oh, so you ruin my career because you want a conversation…' She hesitated because the air between them was potent and she knew it was more than conversation they both craved. It was one of the reasons for her defensiveness because even after everything there remained desire. 'What is Bernadetta going to say when I return home without the contract?'

'You will think of something.'

She stared at him in anger and her lips twisted. 'You know how important work is to me.'

'As I said, I am sure you will think of something. So, how has it been?' he pushed for her to open up. 'Work?'

'Much the same.' Gabi selected a plump fig but as the questions began her appetite faded and she found that she was playing with her food.

'Is it still busy?' he asked, knowing she had just come back from leave.

'Extremely.'

She wasn't going to tell him about the baby, Alim realised. He was almost certain the baby must be his but he had to make sure.

'So what else have you been doing with your time?'

Gabi gave a small mirthless laugh before answering him. 'You've lost any right to ask about my personal life.'

'Have you met someone?' he asked. 'Is that why you are so uncomfortable to be here?'

A piece of fruit had just found its way to her mouth and he watched as she furiously swallowed, such was her haste to respond.

'I'm uncomfortable to be here because of what you did to me,' Gabi said, and she knew that tears flashed in her eyes. She wished she had found a more sophisticated answer but the fact was he had landed her in hell that morning. 'We don't all leap out of one bed and dive into the next. You hurt me, Alim, badly. I get that you might have been bored that night and just filling in time...'

'Never.'

'Don't!' Gabi said, and she stood from the table, tired of any attempt at being polite. She was glad, so glad that there were no staff and they were in the middle of the desert because she could say exactly what was on her mind and as loudly as she chose to! 'You'd had me already, Alim,' she shouted. 'I was fully prepared to leave it at that, to walk out the door and go back to being colleagues, yet you offered me a year. And a job. You made it more! And then you took it away. Did it give you a kick?'

'Gabi...' He tried to take her arms, to contain her, but she shook him off.

'And now you decide that you want to see me again. Well, tough, Alim, I don't want to see you.' Great thick tears were streaming down her cheeks, and they both knew that she lied.

It was torture not to see him and agony to be here. He did not move to hold her; instead, he drew her into his arms and it truly was the lesser of two evils because even resisting she sank into them.

'I did not set out to hurt you,' Alim told her.

He could feel her anger and the frantic beating of her heart and then she spoke. 'But you did.'

So badly.

'That morning I went for breakfast with my father and he told me the diktat had been invoked.'

Gabi frowned as she recalled a conversation that had taken place so many months ago. 'The same ruling that happened to your father and Fleur?'

'The same one.'

'Why couldn't you have told me this that morning, and saved all this hurt and pain?'

'Where?' Alim asked. 'In the hotel foyer?'

'No, you have an entire floor of the Grande Lucia at your disposal.'

'But the laws state that I cannot be alone with a woman I desire unless it is my future bride.'

Desire.

The word made her burn, it made her face feel hot and she wanted to press her cheek into the cool of his robe, so she did.

Yet she could feel the heat from his skin and the thud of his heart as he spoke.

'Even to work alongside you and want you would be forbidden. When I was showing Raul through the hotel and I came into the ballroom and you were there, I knew it was imperative that I leave or I would have broken the rules by which I have been raised. I can only take a lover here in the desert.'

'Are you camped out here, then?' she asked, and looked up. He smiled and for a moment so did Gabi. When she met his eyes, the problems of the world faded; when he smiled like that she forgot the hurt and how cross she was.

'I have been to the desert,' Alim said, 'alone.'

'Oh.'

He looked at her and her cheeks went a bit pink because she wanted to know about his alone time in the desert.

'And when I am here I think of you.'

'And the night we shared?' she asked, because when exhausted, when wretched, when aching for the memory to fade, the image of them taunted and sleep was no relief for he was there in her dreams.

'I think of that night,' Alim said, 'and I think of this.'

'This?'

'Us here together.'

He had been fighting not to bring her here for many months.

He pulled her in tighter so she could feel his arousal. His hand slipped to her back and his fingers explored the top of her spine while still his eyes held hers.

Gabi knew she should resist and not be drawn further under his spell, yet at the same time she told herself it would be the last time.

This was the only time she would be in the desert with him for she would never be tricked into being here again.

His mouth brushed hers and she tried to keep her lips pressed together but as their mouths met again she realised that the feel of him had never left her mind.

Alim's hand came to the back of her head and as he pressed her in he gave her his tongue.

She accepted. Deeply.

And she offered hers.

They tasted and claimed each other again, while his other hand slid to her breast and took its aching weight.

'Just once,' she told him.

And Gabi meant it.

This wasn't like a break in her diet, this was her absolute rule.

'Once?' Alim checked, and his fingers slid between her thighs, sliding along the velvet of her robe and then probing her softly.

He made her feel weak with the promise of more.

'I mean one night,' Gabi said as his tongue made indecent work of her ear as she amended her rules. 'One night and that's it. I shan't be your on-call desert lover, Alim.'

Gabi would be more than his desert lover, Alim thought, though he chose not to enlighten her.

With a child between them, once he married she would be his mistress.

Alim just had to tell her, though he felt no guilt withholding that information.

After all, Gabi held the biggest secret of all.

'Come to bed,' Alim said.

There, he had decided she would tell him.

Whatever it took.

CHAPTER TWELVE

THIS TIME THEY made it to the sleeping area, because Alim had decided it would be a more measured seduction.

He was not used to being lied to, or having vital information withheld from him. Not for long anyway.

Alim took her by the hand and led her there.

The wind played a seductive tune as she stepped into his chamber and they faced each other.

'Here,' Alim said, 'we are not forbidden.'

But it was a forbidden love.

His fingers traced her clavicle and moved the robe down so that her shoulder was bare, and then he did the same on the other side. Alim's hands roamed over her breasts and to the sides of her ribcage as her mouth ached for his kiss and the weight of him on her.

'I have missed you,' Alim told her.

And she could not confess to just how much she had missed him too, for that would leave her exposed and weak to his demands.

'I have thought about you,' Alim said, and he

pointed to the bed. 'There, on that bed, I have thought about you a lot.'

She swallowed at the image he conjured and watched as he freed himself from his robe.

Gabi caught her breath for, to be kind, her mind had dimmed his beauty a touch, but now it was hers to witness again.

She put a hand up and touched his chest—solid and warm. She pressed her fingers to his skin and then shared a deep kiss as her fingers pressed into the flesh of his torso.

'Have you thought of me?' he asked.

'At first,' Gabi said. 'But I'm over you now.'

'Not quite,' he said, pulling the robe down over her breasts and hips so that it fell to the floor. His hands were thorough and hungry for her body as they again felt her generous flesh.

'Tell me how you have been,' he said as he kissed her all over, gently lowering her so she lay naked on soft silks, 'since you got over me.'

'I've been...' She hesitated, and she wondered what he would say if she told him that each night she still cried herself to sleep. 'Fine.'

'Fine,' he said as he joined her and they lay with their fingers tracing each other's outlines. His muscular arms were as she remembered and his erection still responded to the trace of her finger on the hairs of his thigh. It was Alim who wavered from the sensual tracing and ran his hand along the soft insides of her thighs. He savoured them again with a teasing caress, then tortured her by halting her at the peak of the thrill.

'Did you ever think of contacting me?' he asked, and she bit on her lip in frustration. As he held back the pleasure, she became a little more truthful. 'I wanted to but, you moved to Zethlehan.'

'Not until recently.' He looked up. 'You had months when you could have made contact.'

'For the pleasure of being rejected again?' Gabi shot back, and her more honest response was rewarded by a deep kiss to her breast, one that hurt because it was so exquisite.

His fingers stroked her inside and it was his deep desire for her that made Gabi burn and want.

Yet as he removed his fingers and the deep contact of his mouth, she was reminded how abruptly he had ended things between them and as he went to part her legs, she drew them closed.

He parted them with his palm. Not even a hint of pressure, just the soft touch of his skin and she opened to Alim; he came to kneel between her calves.

She felt again like his prey.

He moved her knees and her legs up higher, and her throat was tight as he lowered his head.

'Gabi…' he said, and she felt his words in her most intimate space. 'Tell me…'

Tell him what?

That she loved him and that she was going out of her mind because she lay in the desert with a man who had brought her here on a lie? Yet she was fighting not to plead for him.

His tongue was subtle.

At first.

She considered that she might relax into the caress of his mouth and then his kiss strengthened and he moved down onto his stomach, his tongue slipping inside her. She heard the kiss and swallow of him and she moaned.

'Tell me...' he said again.

'I have thought of you.'

There, she had said it.

His tongue was making love to her and his fingers hurt her thighs but she would not have him lighten his touch, not even a fraction.

Gabi's hand was turning, searching, for a pillow, a cushion, for an anchor but he was tasting her so deeply her fingers then tugged at his silky hair. His unshaven jaw was rough and delicious and she had never thought she would know such pleasure again.

'Alim...'

Inadvertently, as she had the night their baby had been born, she sobbed out his name.

Alim liked it.

He liked how she cried out his name as she started to come, and he drank her in, yet she frustrated him too for, even in the throes of passion she did not reveal the truth.

And so he rose from between her legs, left her in the middle of her climax, and reached for a sheath.

Gabi almost screamed in frustration at the sudden dearth of sensation. He rose over her and she ached for him to be inside her, yet he was busy taking the care he had not that first night.

'Please…' Gabi begged, and she was about to tell him she was covered, not to worry, for she was on the Pill, but it didn't matter now; he was over her and squeezing into where she was so swollen, aching and ripe.

'We don't want you getting pregnant…' he said, and she gave in to the bliss, but it was short-lived, for Gabi's eyes flew open to just one word from Alim.

'Again…'

He knew!

She was a ball of panic and he was taking her, a mire of sensation, for he was an assault on all of her senses.

His lovemaking was savage. Her pleasure he had taken care of already and now, when perhaps it should be just for him, she was taken to the edge of sanity as Alim unleashed himself.

He spoke words she did not understand but they were harsh and scolding, yet his arms held her tight as he bucked within.

She was dragging her nails down his back and now it was Gabi's anger that was released. For he had left her, and she had had to fight to survive in a world that did not contain him.

Their teeth clashed, their bodies locked and she bit his shoulder; it felt primal and she was screaming. Her thighs burned now as her legs wrapped tightly around him, and his rapid thrusts had her high and coming so deeply as he shot into her.

'Never…' he said, and was about to tell her to never lie again, but as he came, as he felt her deep pulses drag him in, words did not matter.

He lay on top of her and they breathed in air that felt clear and cool, as if a storm had just passed.

It had.

Alim knew, Gabi thought as she lay there.

He kissed her back, a very soft kiss, for the storm really had passed.

She knew he knew now.

CHAPTER THIRTEEN

'WERE YOU EVER going to tell me?'

Alim had waited for her breath to even out before he asked her.

'Yes.'

'I don't believe you,' Alim said, and he turned his face to Gabi's. 'I gave you every opportunity and you said nothing.'

'I wanted to tell you from a distance.'

'Why?'

Gabi didn't answer that for she did not want to admit that being around him made her feel weak and that she'd been scared what she might agree to when she lay by his side.

Here, she felt they could do no wrong.

Here, in the desert, this love did not feel so forbidden, and the idea of being his desert lover felt rather wonderful, in fact.

'What did we have?'

His words said so much—that he accepted their baby as his and that the question was gently asked brought tears to her eyes.

'A little girl.'

She was back there again in those lonely hours, giving birth without Alim by her side, but now his hand found hers as she told him their daughter's name.

'I called her Lucia.'

'She is well?'

Gabi nodded for her words were strangled by tears as she heard the care behind his questions.

'You'll never forgive me, will you?'

'Gabi, I accept that the decision would have felt like an impossible one.'

Alim did not like it and maybe later he would resent the times denied to them but now was not that time; there were too many things he needed to know this moment.

'When did you have her?'

'The last time we met,' Gabi said. 'When you were showing Raul through the hotel.'

Alim frowned. 'The night I returned to Zethlehan?'

Gabi nodded.

'You didn't look pregnant,' Alim said. 'Though admittedly I was doing all I could not to look at you.'

'I lost a lot of weight,' Gabi told him. 'I've put it all back on, though.'

'Good.'

He was the most back-to-front man she knew, for he was playing with her stomach as if it was the most beautiful stomach in the world.

'I was sick a lot at first and then I was very busy

with work. I was just about to go on leave when I went into labour.'

'That would have been far too soon.'

'She's done so well, though,' Gabi said. 'Lucia amazed the doctor and nurses; she was early but so strong.'

'The al-Lehans are.' One day he would tell her about the strong lineage; one day he would share in tales of babies that should not have survived but had lived to rule.

But not now.

For Alim ached with sadness that a desert princess had been born but his country would never know her name.

She did not exist as his daughter, except here in the desert.

Gabi had left the bed and had gone to her case in the hallway and retrieved her tablet.

There was something so splendid about her, Alim thought as she walked back to the bed. He knew Gabi was shy, yet here she was not and he loved how she slipped back to his side; he wrapped an arm around her as she opened up the latest image of Lucia—the one that her mother had sent her just as she had landed here in Zethlehan.

There had never been any real doubt in his mind, Alim had known she was his, but he had never expected to feel so moved by a photo.

Her eyes were almond shaped and she was a beautiful old soul, a true al-Lehan.

'When was this taken?' Alim asked.

'My mother sent it to me yesterday. I got it when we landed.'

'She is tiny,' he said, unable to take his eyes from his daughter and loathing that he could only see her on a screen.

'She's the size of a newborn now,' Gabi said. 'She caught up quickly.'

He scrolled through the images and Gabi explained each one. 'That was the day I brought her home from the hospital,' she said. 'And that's on the night she was born.'

He had been on his way here.

Alim looked at their fragile daughter and then at the mother who held her. Gabi had indeed lost weight; in the picture she looked drawn and pale, scared yet proud as she looked down at her very new daughter, and his heart twisted in fear and pain as he thought of how it could have gone.

'You have done well,' Alim said, and looked at Gabi.

She had expected him to be accusatory, to be furious for all she had denied him, yet his voice was kind and his words told her he was proud of her for the care that their daughter had received.

Yes, from the day she had met him he had enthralled her, for his responses were like no others; they threw her in new directions.

And then he turned back to the tablet and the photos of his daughter. 'That's all there are…' Gabi said.

Except there was another image that held his attention now—the one of Gabi and him dancing in the deserted ballroom.

She blushed. It felt as if he was looking through her diary and she hastily moved to play the image down.

'The photographer had left a time-lapse camera set up, there was this at the end…' She was a little embarrassed to have saved it, but how could she be when she now lay in his bed and from that night they had made a daughter?

'I'll send you the pictures of Lucia—'

'Already done,' Alim said, as he clicked on them.

They lay there in the dark with the wind an orchestra that seemed to play only for them.

'Will you bring her next time?' Alim asked, and Gabi went still, for there would not be a next time.

Nothing had changed for Gabi, except that he knew.

'Has James ever been to Zethlehan?' she asked, instead of answering.

'No.'

'In case it caused rumours to spread?'

'There are always rumours and they are dealt with by the palace,' Alim said. 'No, James has never been here because Fleur always refused to come.'

'She's never been?'

'No. Fleur said that she deserved better than a tent in the desert so my father saw that she and James had a home in London and an apartment in Rome.'

'At the Grande Lucia?'

'No. They have only started to dine there since I bought it.' He gave her a smile. 'It is there that James and Mona met—she was there for her grandparents' wedding anniversary and Fleur and James were there with my father.'

That's right, she remembered Mona telling her that and it had seemed so inconsequential at the time.

'I don't want to be your lover, Alim.'

'You would be better than a lover,' Alim told her. 'You would be my mistress.'

He said it as if it were a reward.

'I don't want to be like Fleur,' Gabi said. 'I don't want to bring her here and...' Yet she fought with herself, for even as she said it, she lied.

There was nothing she wanted more right now than for Lucia to lie between them.

There was nothing that appealed more than the thought of visiting Alim, and their child growing up with the love of her father.

'Would it be such a terrible life?' he turned and asked her. 'I would take care of you two so well.'

She stared back at him.

'You could come here often and still have your career.'

'Career?' She gave a short, incredulous laugh. 'I seem to remember you offering me that once before; it didn't last very long.'

The hurt was still there—even recalling that moment took her straight back to the pain he had caused her. 'Anyway, the Grande Lucia has been sold...'

'The contracts are not signed yet.'

And it didn't appease her—because Bastiano was his friend, but that meant little to Alim, she was sure.

He was ruthless and would get his own way.

Well, not in this.

'I don't want to work for you,' Gabi said, and her voice was certain. 'I want my own career.'

'And you could have it. I would see you often.'

'Where?'

'Mostly here,' Alim said. 'And once things were more settled for my country I could spend more time with you and Lucia in Rome…'

'You mean once you are married and have an heir?'

'Yes.'

And even if it appalled her, it was the life he had been born to, Gabi knew.

'You didn't approve when it was your father,' she pointed out.

'I did not know then that they had made things work.' And he told her a little about how he had found out his mother was happier than he had believed she was.

'I think we could do it even better than them.'

He made the unpalatable sweet, for now the winds buffeted the walls of the desert tent and she could almost imagine a little family here at times. But then her eyes closed on the madness that her mind proposed she consider; she saw the image of Fleur sitting taking refreshments alone; she thought of the other injured parties that an illicit love brought.

'I wouldn't do that to your wife,' Gabi said. 'And I shan't do it to our child.'

'You'd deny her a chance to be with her father?'

'Never,' Gabi said. 'You can come and see her whenever you choose.'

She was braver in words than in thought, not that he gave her a moment to think.

'I want you to move into the Grande Lucia.'

'It's about to be sold.'

'Bastiano isn't going to be kicking out the guests… you're to move there forthwith.'

'No.' He was pulling her into his world, and she would not allow it. 'I shan't be your lover and I shan't be your mistress.' She rolled onto her side and faced away from him.

'Gabi, just think about it.'

'No.' She was crying because he made her weaken. 'Haven't you heard a word I've said?'

'I heard all that you said,' Alim told her as he spooned in from behind, his hand on her stomach and his mouth at her ear, 'but I think we need to speak at more length.'

The only length she was certain of was the one that was nudging between her thighs and Gabi knew it would soon be the delicious experience all over again.

Not just now but for the rest of her life.

'No, I need to get back to my baby.'

She felt lost and reckless to be in the desert with him, and her mind was made up.

'I shan't be your mistress.'

Gabi's mind was *almost* made up but she was open to persuasion in his arms. And so she climbed out of the vast bed before she shattered again to his touch.

'Get back into bed,' Alim said.

He lay uncovered and beautiful and she had never fought harder not to simply give in to his demands. 'The only way I'll sleep with you again is as your wife.'

'Wife?' Alim's tone told her how impossible that was. 'I am offering you—'

'I don't want to be your mistress, Alim.'

'Please,' he angrily retorted. 'You want centuries of history wiped out just for you?'

A few months ago she would have backed down, almost apologised for being so bold.

Yet what they had found together had changed her, and for the better.

She had a baby to think of too.

His love, though not on offer, made her strong.

'I don't just want it,' Gabi hotly responded. 'I insist on it.'

'Oh, you do, do you?'

'Yes, and now I want to leave.'

He just lay there.

'I said—'

'I heard.'

He rolled over and the world was invading because here in their remote haven Alim retrieved his phone.

'The helicopter will be here within the hour.'

Gabi breathed out in relief, but her relief was short-lived.

'Now,' he said, 'get back to bed.'

CHAPTER FOURTEEN

OH, IT SHOULD feel wonderful to be back in Rome and to step into her mother's house and hold Lucia.

She brought her baby back to her flat and drew the drapes on the world to create her own little haven of peace.

But peace was fragile and, Gabi knew, at any moment it could be, *would* be, shattered.

That much Gabi was certain of.

The days passed and she heard nothing from Alim, but the lack of contact did not serve as relief.

She knew he was working his way towards them.

Indefinable, indescribable.

Gabi just knew.

For seven mornings, the sun rose as promised in the east and for seven nights it slipped away into the west, but distance and time did not soothe Gabi. She knew that Alim kept his family close—his insistence at maintaining ties to his half-brother James, despite his father's pressure to leave well alone, told Gabi that.

And Lucia was his daughter.

Always Alim seemed a step ahead of her, and Gabi, rather than trying to second-guess his next move, decided to focus on her own.

If she was going to be strong against Alim, then she needed a life. She needed to be able to take care of her daughter enough that she did not solely depend on him, and that started now.

'I'd hoped for something more concrete!' Bernadetta was less than impressed with the rather sparse report Gabi offered as to her time in Zethlehan.

'When is the wedding?'

'Sultan Alim is not sure,' Gabi answered, and then she looked at Bernadetta. 'I've been thinking, Bernadetta…' Except that sounded unsure. 'As you know,' Gabi amended, 'for a long time I've wanted to go out on my own…'

'Oh, not this again.' Bernadetta rolled her eyes. 'Do I have to remind you of the terms—?'

'Bernadetta,' Gabi broke in, 'I cannot hire any of your contacts for six months, I'm very aware of that, but they can still hire me.'

'Hire you?' Bernadetta gave a condescending laugh.

'Rosa would hire me in an instant. I worked for her for ages and, to be honest, with Lucia so young the thought of more regular hours for a few months is appealing. And, of course, some of Rosa's brides-to-be might not yet have found a wedding planner…' She could see Bernadetta's rapid blink but she quickly recovered.

'You wouldn't last five minutes in this industry without me.'

'I think I'll last a whole lot longer,' Gabi said. 'I guess we're going to find out, but not for a while, though. I've just returned from maternity leave so I'm legally obliged—'

'Gabi,' Bernadetta broke in, 'this is nonsense. We've got a royal wedding coming up—'

'We?' Gabi checked. It was the first time she had ever included Gabi in the business and it had taken a threat to resign to hear it. 'Matrimoni di Bernadetta has a potential contract. I have a child to raise. Bernadetta, I think we could make a very strong partnership but obviously it has to be something that would work for you too.'

'Gabi,' Bernadetta said, 'you're getting ideas above your station.'

'No.' Gabi shook her head. 'I've got ideas and plenty of them, and they're exactly where they ought to be.'

It didn't go well.

She wasn't exactly laughed out of the office, as Gabi had predicted she would be; instead Bernadetta sulked and ignored her.

In Zethlehan it wasn't business as usual either.

Violetta asked to see Alim and broke the news.

'Bastiano Conti has withdrawn his offer.'

Usually Alim would hold onto a hiss of indignation when a sale fell through at this late stage. He never revealed his emotions, even to the most trusted staff or those closest in his circle.

Now, though, he let out an audible sigh.

One of relief.

He did not want the Grande Lucia to be sold.

Alim loved that building; there had been more than memories made there and he did not want that chapter of his life closed.

Lucia.

He had to see her.

'What was his reason?' Alim asked Violetta.

'Apparently one of your chambermaids has light fingers. A family heirloom was stolen from Bastiano.'

'I will deal with that,' Alim said.

He and Bastiano were friends, and a deal falling through would not mar that.

Business was kept separate, but still he rang the hotel and asked to be put through to the head of Housekeeping to find out things for himself before calling Bastiano.

'Young Sophie…' Benita told him. 'I wanted to give her the benefit of the doubt but a ring was found when she turned out the pockets of her uniform so there was no choice but to let her go.'

Sophie was a friend of Gabi's, Alim knew.

He had often seen them chatting; in days long gone he had seen them with their coats on at the end of the day, heading out for supper.

And, on Gabi's behalf, he probed further.

'Did she admit to it?' Alim checked.

'Of course not,' Benita said. 'I've yet to find a thief who would.'

'Yes but—'

'Alim,' Benita said, 'I think there might have been something between our esteemed guest and maid.'

'Oh.'

'It's been dealt with.'

'Okay.'

Yet he could not let his thoughts of the Grande Lucia go.

He was flicking through his phone, looking at pictures of Lucia, and then he came to the photo of him with Lucia's mother.

It was a magnificent portrait of a couple gazing at each other, on the edge of a future together...

And Alim felt his heart quicken.

He reached for the leather-bound folder on his desk and read the pertinent parts of the diktat.

And then he read the rest.

Violetta brought in refreshments but instead of waving her out he had her bring him more files.

Ancient files with ancient rulings that he had been forced to learn as a child.

Alim studied them as a man now.

He read the ancient teachings and pored over the laws of his land, and as he turned the pages Alim glanced up and saw his father standing there.

They were barely speaking.

His father considered Alim to be stubborn.

'I have chosen my bride,' Alim told his father.

'That decision belongs to me,' Oman said, for he knew the laws well.

'Then you had better make sure that it is the right one,' Alim responded coolly, but his voice held a silk-clad threat, 'or there shall be no wedding.'

Oman's assessment was the correct one.

Sultan Alim al-Lehan of Zethlehan was the most stubborn man in this land.

He would not succumb to rules of old, as his father had.

Alim would work within them.

CHAPTER FIFTEEN

GABI NEVER FORGOT.

Even as she sat in her tiny flat, consoling poor Sophie, Alim was not far from her mind.

For nearly a week, Sophie had been around every day bemoaning the loss of her job and the man who had caused it—Bastiano Conti.

'I would never steal,' Sophie said. 'But if I did, I would not steal some stupid emerald and pearl ring. It would be diamonds.'

She made Gabi laugh, and in the second that the world felt lighter, Alim invaded, for her phone rang and the fragile peace was shattered.

'Why,' Alim asked, 'are you still living in that flat, when there is an apartment at the Grande Lucia at your disposal?'

She gave an apologetic smile to Sophie and went through to her bedroom to take the call.

Lucia was asleep in her crib and Gabi kept her voice down so as not to disturb her, and also because she did not want Sophie to hear.

'Because I refuse to be kept by you.'

'Your daughter has a father who will provide for her.' Alim gave in, he refused to argue on the phone when he would see Gabi soon, but there was something he badly needed to know.

'How is Lucia?'

'She slept through last night for the first time.'

'That is good. I am in Rome and I would like to meet her.'

Gabi screwed her eyes closed.

She had been dreading this, had been preparing herself for this moment. He had told her that nothing would stop him from seeing his child, and yet again Alim was a step ahead for she had at least thought there would be time to prepare for their meeting.

'When?'

'This afternoon. Is that a problem for you?'

'No,' Gabi admitted. 'I've got a couple of days off.'

'Really?'

'Bernadetta told me not to come in this weekend,' Gabi said. 'I'm not sure if I've been fired. I asked Bernadetta for a partnership…'

Alim, it would seem, had lost interest in her career plans for he spoke over Gabi. 'Can you bring Lucia to me at the Grande Lucia at one?'

She looked around her home; no, she could not imagine him here.

'For how long?'

'The afternoon,' Alim answered calmly. 'Say, until five?'

No, *that* was the part she dreaded, for Gabi knew she would have to get over him all over again.

Sophie was terribly hard to get rid of, but Gabi pulled out an excuse and, sounding like Bernadetta, told her friend that she had a migraine.

'That came on quickly,' Sophie said.

'Yes, they tend to.'

Thankfully Sophie soon left and, wishing she could lie down in a darkened room and hide from the world for a while, Gabi bathed her slippery baby and washed her hair and then she fed her.

'You're going to meet your daddy,' Gabi told her.

And though Gabi was worried for herself, and her absolute drop-knickers reaction to Alim, at least today she had the shield of her daughter. Alim would be far too besotted with Lucia to worry about other things.

And, more importantly, she was so happy for Lucia.

No, history was not repeating itself—this little girl would have a dad.

Of sorts.

And so, just before one, Gabi walked into the foyer of the Grande Lucia, as she had done many, many times, but then she stopped in her tracks.

The pillar display in the middle of the foyer was no longer its trademark red. Instead, there was a stunning display of sweet peas.

Pinks, lilacs and creams, they were absolutely stunning and she stood for a moment, enjoying the wonderful change.

'They're for you,' Gabi said to her daughter. 'He did this for you!'

Her happiness soon evaporated, though. She was met by Violetta, and it would seem that both baby and mother required preparation to enter the Sultan's world.

Pride had ensured that Gabi had dressed as well as she could for today, and little Lucia was wearing a gorgeous outfit and was wrapped in a new muslin square.

It wasn't enough.

And it wasn't just Lucia who had to be prepared.

There was a silver robe laid out for Gabi and, she quickly realised, Violetta had an assistant to do her make-up and hair.

'That won't be necessary,' Gabi said. 'I'm here so that Alim can see his baby.'

'The Sultan—' Violetta started, but Gabi would not hear it.

'He didn't tell me he was a sultan when he took me to bed,' Gabi interrupted. 'And I am not here as his mistress. I am here as the mother of his child.'

Violetta blinked, clearly more used to people bending over backwards to please the Sultan. Well, no bending over would be happening today.

'This is Hannan,' Violetta introduced them. 'She is a royal nanny of considerable standing and will help get the baby ready to meet Sultan Alim.'

'Her name is Lucia,' Gabi said. 'And she *is* ready.'

This time Violetta paid no attention.

The muslin was replaced with a cashmere wrap

and Gabi bit her lip as Hannan dared check that her baby was clean enough for the Sultan's eyes.

It incensed Gabi but for now she stayed quiet.

Lucia did not.

She let out a cry of protest as her face was wiped.

'Perhaps we will wait till after she is fed so that she is content when she sees the Sultan,' Hannan suggested.

'She isn't due to be fed for another three hours.' Gabi said. 'And, given I'm due to leave at five, it would make it a very short first visit with her father.'

'Perhaps just a small feed,' Hannan suggested. 'The Sultan is not yet here.'

Gabi clutched her daughter, and already ached for her, unable to believe that Alim could be late for his first meeting with his daughter.

The wait was awful.

But finally the words were said. 'The Sultan is ready for you.'

The real question was, was *she* ready to face Alim?

His offer that she be his mistress had been met with the contempt it deserved.

Yet talking to herself was easy when Alim wasn't close.

She picked up little Lucia and held her close and when Hannan came over to check again that her baby was sweet and clean enough to meet her father for the first time, Gabi shot her a look.

Wisely, Hannan stepped back.

The small entourage walked along the long carpeted corridor and Gabi did her best not to think of the last time she had been here—being kissed up against these walls, falling together through the door that Violetta now knocked on.

Making love.

She walked in, holding Lucia to her chest, with Violetta and Hannan by her side.

Alim stood by a window in his immaculate reception room. The fire that had blazed as he'd stripped her naked was now devoid of flames and filled with an autumnal floral display.

A tamed version of itself.

Just like Alim.

He was wearing a suit and was clean shaven, and though he looked somewhat less formidable out of traditional robes, not for a moment would she forget his power.

'I apologise for keeping you waiting,' he said by way of introduction, but offered no explanation for the reason he had done so. He looked over at Violetta and Hannan. 'Excuse us, please.' Polite, in all dealings *outside* the bedroom, Alim dismissed his staff and Gabi stood, a little awkwardly, as Alim's eyes flicked down to the baby she held in her arms, though he did not approach.

'She's just been fed,' Gabi said with a distinct edge to her voice, 'to ensure that she's no trouble for you.'

'Did they feed you too?' Alim asked, implying he knew full well that it was the mother who was trouble, and he saw that she resisted a smile.

'No,' Gabi said.

'Then I had better watch out.'

Indeed he had, for Gabi made her own rules, and that, his father had pointed out, might make her an unwise choice for a sultan's bride.

He walked over and peered at the bundle that she held—their tiny baby hidden in a swathe of cashmere.

Gabi watched as his hand moved back the fabric. She heard the slight hitch in his breath as, for the first time, he met his daughter.

She had dark hair, like her parents', and her dark lashes swept over round cheeks. Her little rosebud mouth was pink and her skin as pale as Gabi's.

And she was beautiful.

Alim had been raised knowing he would one day be Sultan of Sultans, yet he met true responsibility now, for he would move mountains for his daughter and she had not even opened her eyes to look at him.

He looked up to Gabi and saw that *her* eyes were angry.

Though she held Lucia tenderly, Gabi's stance was almost confrontational, and he loved that she would do anything to protect not just her daughter but herself.

She was a wise choice indeed.

And for Gabi he *had* moved mountains.

Though Alim would tell her that later, right now he was overwhelmed to see Lucia.

'Can I hold her?'

Gabi handed him their child and it was the first awkward move she had ever seen him make.

Indeed, it was awkward at first, for Lucia was so light and she moved and stirred as she went into her father's arms, and he held her perhaps a little too firmly.

Gabi said nothing; she did not tell him to watch her head and she did not move to hush her daughter, who was starting to wakeup; instead, she walked over and took a seat.

She was close to tears, watching him hold their daughter so tenderly and witnessing the obvious love he had for Lucia.

It didn't feel fair that they could never be a family. She wanted to go over to where he took a seat, she wanted to be with the two people she loved.

His part-time lover.

The desert still tempted her. Alim always would.

Then Lucia opened her eyes.

Alim had never doubted that Lucia was his—had he, though, he would have been proved a fool, for her eyes were navy, turning to grey, and there were the same silver flecks that greeted him in the mirror each morning.

He hoped she might cry so that he could hand her back to her mother, for he had never felt more moved than now; there was guilt too for the months Gabi had dealt with this alone, and fear about how tiny Lucia was, even though she was more than three months old.

But Lucia did not cry or whimper. She looked

straight at her daddy and smiled and completely won his heart.

'I could have lived my entire life not knowing about her.'

'No,' Gabi said. 'I lived my life without knowing my father so I would never do that to my child. I was going to wait till I felt a little better, and then tell you.'

'Better?' He frowned, worried that she had been ill.

'Stronger.'

'Stronger?' Alim checked.

'To say no to you.'

His eyes raised just a fraction, as if doubting she could.

'I meant what I said—I shan't be your mistress, Alim. I will always let you see your daughter whenever you come here to Rome but there will be no trips to the desert.'

'Really?'

'Yes.'

She must be stronger because she almost believed that she could say no to him.

'So you are going to be single and—'

'I didn't say that,' Gabi corrected. 'You will marry the bride of the Sultan of Sultans's choosing and I will get on with my life. I won't be like Fleur, living a lonely life with you as my occasional, discreet lover.'

'Oh, so you hope to meet someone else?'

'Yes.'

He stared at her and she tried not to meet his gaze because she just could not imagine being with another man.

Ever.

She could not imagine anyone after him, yet she had to believe it, for she would not be his mistress, neither would she be alone.

The minutes passed so slowly they were half an hour in with three more to go.

He picked up a phone and soon Hannan appeared; Gabi's lips tightened as she scooped up Lucia and took her away, and soon it was just the two of them.

'I thought you wanted to see her.'

'I don't need to stare at her for the entire visit to love her. I will call for refreshments for you.'

They made small talk as they waited for afternoon tea to arrive.

'Bernadetta is being weird,' Gabi said. 'She won't take my calls.'

He just shrugged and then told her his news. 'I have withdrawn the Grande Lucia from sale.'

'I thought the contracts were signed.'

'No. Bastiano returned to the Grande Lucia for a visit and apparently some jewellery was stolen from his suite—your friend apparently.'

Gabi wasn't going to blush or apologise for Sophie. She just gave a shrug.

'He's withdrawn his offer.'

And now Gabi rolled her eyes because Alim would be here in Rome so much more.

Her desire was safer from a distance.

Arabian teas, coffees and pastries arrived and as the maid poured Alim declined.

'Enjoy,' Alim said to Gabi as the maid left.

'Where are you going?'

'Bed,' Alim answered. 'I read that you should try and sleep when the baby does.'

Her mouth twisted into an incredulous smile when she thought of the hours she had paced the floor with her baby and snatched twenty-minute naps on the sofa.

He had not a clue!

'Half an hour of fatherhood and you're already tired?' Gabi accused.

'Months of fatherhood, had I but known,' Alim corrected. 'And months of abstinence, apart from one night in the desert.'

And he took her back in her mind to where she had been trying to avoid going.

Gabi looked ahead and tried not to think of her time in his bed.

And Alim, as he stepped into the bedroom where he had had so much planned, instead was incensed by her words.

Pride perhaps was at fault, but there was also this need to know not that Lucia was his but that *Gabi* was his—that he was and always would be her one and only.

He started to undress and then remembered he should be dressed for the planned proposal and standing when Gabi inevitably walked in.

Surprise!

Yet she did not walk in.

Alim rarely got angry, he rarely cared enough to be so.

And he was also jealous.

Gabi had riled him.

On what should be the most romantic of days she spoke of other men!

Oh, Alim wanted to prove her wrong. There would *never* be others.

So, instead of the plans he had made, Alim opened the bedside drawer and there they lay his collection of diamonds; he selected the best, then he closed the drapes and turned off the lights.

He would not be brought to his knees until Gabi was.

And so he walked out.

She sat, drinking tea.

Her foot was tapping, Alim noticed, but apart from that she seemed calm, like a guest sitting in the foyer, waiting for her car to arrive, or to be told that her suite was now ready.

Gabi was not calm.

She had been fighting with herself not to follow him in.

To 'Keep Calm and Drink Tea', as suggested.

Yet her hands were shaking and her desire was fierce and she ached for these visiting hours to be over.

For an imaginary nurse to come in and ring a bell so that she could leave.

Then he walked out.

The jacket was off, the tie gone and his shirt half-undone, as if he had been undressing and had suddenly remembered something.

Indeed he had. 'There will be others?' Alim questioned, and even though his voice was dark it held a slightly mocking edge, for he was sure there could be no other.

And what was said now would define their future, Gabi knew.

She would not be Fleur, sitting in the foyer of this very hotel and ignored. She would not be his mistress and make love and then not make a fuss when he returned to his wife.

How bloody dare he?

And so she met his eyes and she played a very dangerous game with a sultan who was already not best pleased.

'Maybe just *one* other,' Gabi said. 'Perhaps I will find the love of my life.'

'What if you have already found him?' Alim said.

'How can I have,' Gabi countered, 'when he speaks of a future wife?'

And she found out then just how strong she was because now she could look him in the eye and tell him things she would once never have dared. Now she stood her ground and it felt firm beneath her feet, for she was resolute.

She watched as he reached into his pocket and beside her teacup he placed a stone.

A magnificent one.

'You shall be kept in splendour,' Alim said, and when every other woman would reach for the stone, she had the nerve to take a sip of her tea. 'Never again speak of other men. Now,' Alim said by way of parting, 'come to bed.'

She would not succumb.

Gabi stood, walked across the lounge and looked out of the window.

A bridal car was pulling up outside the church further down the street and she watched as a bride was helped out and her dress arranged.

The little flower girl stood patiently as Gabi's heart impatiently beat for the day that it might be her.

Never the bride.

She had never been able to envisage herself as one.

And now she knew why.

A mistress was all she would ever be.

No!

Gabi was torn for as she watched the bride walk into the church she told herself that a mistress was surely better than being a virtual spinster, holding onto just two perfect nights for the rest of her life.

That was all her love life would be.

For, despite brave words she might say to Alim, in truth, there would never be another man—Gabi had already found the love of her life.

Yet agreeing to be his mistress went against everything she believed in, and if even the thought of it was eating her up, living it would be unbearable.

Neither was she cut out to keep secrets, for she would want to sing their love to the world, and she was hardly of a size that faded neatly into the background.

No, Gabi would not be his mistress, but that did not stop the door to his bedroom calling her.

Set your limits.

Alim's words now replayed to her.

Do only what you are prepared to do. What works for you...

And Gabi knew what did.

Alim.

CHAPTER SIXTEEN

GABI WALKED OVER to a dresser and took some paper and wrote down three little words.

No, thank you.

She placed them by the stone that Alim had left out for her.

Gabi would not be kept.

She would not be another Fleur, paid for in diamonds, rich in everything save respect.

Then she undressed and, naked, walked to the closed doors of the bedroom.

She would not cry and she would not be a martyr as she took those final steps, for Gabi wanted this.

Gabi stepped into darkness. The air was fragrant and sweet but there was the now familiar musky note of Alim and the pull of arousal as she came to the side of the bed.

'What kept you?' Alim asked.

'My thoughts.'

'And they are?'

'That I'll never be your mistress.'

'Then why *are* you here?' Alim asked as his hands roamed her naked body.

'I shall be your lover,' Gabi told him, and she knelt on the bed and kissed his salty chest. 'I will be your lover in the desert at times and at others I will be your lover in Rome.'

And when once she had been demure, she was not so much now, for she wanted to intimately taste every inch of him. Gabi kissed down his stomach and between hot kisses she told him how it would be.

'I don't want your diamonds, I owe you nothing.'

And in the dark she could not see his smile, for he loved it that she stood up to him.

'But I do want the contract for your wedding,' Gabi said, and she blew onto his wet skin as his fingers dug into her thigh. 'I'm going to stand there and you can damn well watch what you're saying goodbye to, because your mistress I shall never be.'

His scent was her addiction and her undoing; she could feel him against her cheek and so she took him in her hand and tasted him.

She took him deep; his hands went into her hair and his hips rose at the bliss of unskilled but willing lips and to the heat of her tongue.

And then he pulled her up before he came, yet still she told him how it would be.

'The day your bride is chosen I'll cease to be your lover.'

Gabi had not finished school, neither was she

versed in the rules, yet she, Alim knew, was as clever and as powerful as he.

He pulled her up to his kiss and as their tongues touched he lowered Gabi onto him.

The relief of him inside her was unrivalled.

A future she could now see.

He held her hips and they found their rhythm. She danced as if free, for that was how she felt when they were together.

She wanted the light on, she ached to see him, but as she leant and reached for the bedside lamp his hand grabbed at hers. Gabi lost her stride and toppled forward. There was a tussle and he flipped her and then entered her again, and she lay in the dark, being taken.

Gabi did not bring him to his knees but to his forearms.

'Yes,' Alim said as he thrust into her. 'You *shall* be at my wedding.'

'Alim…' Gabi sobbed, for she had meant it as a threat yet it seemed to turn him on.

It was the way she said his name that called to him. Like a plea from the soul. And when Gabi said it again he came hard into her. She fought not to, Gabi really did—fought not to cave to the flood of warmth and want and the orbit of them.

She lost.

Near spent, Alim had the pleasure of the full clutch of her passion and his body pinned her as she writhed, and when she wanted to breathe it was the only need his body denied her, for he then took the air from the room.

'You shall be at my wedding…as my bride.'

She was always a little dizzy when Alim was close—for Gabi it was a constant state of affairs. Held in his arms, breathing his scent, and her body still coming down from the high he so readily gave, she told herself she had misheard him.

And then light invaded for Alim reached over and turned on the bedside lamp and his bedroom was not as she recalled it.

There were flowers.

Sweet peas.

Ten thousand of them, she was sure, and the flowers in the foyer had, in fact, been for her.

But that was not all.

A stunning portrait had been blown up and set on an easel beside the bed.

It was the image of them.

Alim had moved more than mountains, he had turned back the hands of time. For days he had pored over the rules he had studied for years, searching, discounting and trying to find a way to make it work for them.

'You and Lucia are the most wonderful things that have ever happened to me,' Alim told her.

'According to your land, we *never* happened.'

'No.' Alim shook his head. 'When the Sultan offers a commitment it is to be taken seriously…' He took her in his arms. 'I committed to you that night.'

'You offered a year.'

'I vowed fidelity.'

He had.

'And unless it has been broken, you are still mine.'

'Alim?'

'There has been no one else,' Alim said. 'There could be no one else. Had you not spoken of other men you would have walked into this room and I would have got down on my knees and asked you to be my wife.'

Gabi laughed.

Still dizzy, still confused, she laughed, because even if he had planned the perfect proposal she would not change how it had transpired.

There was nothing about them she would change.

Even now, could she go back to their first night and be on the Pill, she would not. There was nothing she would change save for the cruel rules of his land, and now her laughter died.

'Your father will never agree.'

'Reluctantly, very reluctantly, he already has.' Now it was Alim who smiled. 'I am more stubborn than he. I went through the rules and the diktat and then I showed him this image. I told my father that there had been no one else and that that would remain the case, for the rest of my life if need be.'

'I don't understand.'

'My father caved in to the Sultan of Sultans' demands when Fleur would not come to the desert. I told him that I would not.'

And still she did not understand.

'We think the same, Gabi. For the decision you reached was mine too. We would have more than made it as lovers. I would have come to Italy regularly, and brought you on occasion to the desert, and you would have remained the one and only woman in my life.'

And she stared back at him as he told her just how deep his love was.

'I told my father that if he did not choose you as my bride, then I would never marry. Kaleb is next in line, Yasmin after that, and they will one day have children. The country is not short of heirs...'

'You told him that you'd give up your throne?'

'No.' Alim shook his head. 'I would still rule, but they would be my heirs.'

He had thought every detail through and he had presented it to his father, just as he would in any business meeting.

Only this one involved his heart.

'He knows I am strong, and he knows his own regrets. He agreed.'

'And Lucia...' Gabi asked. 'What will your people think?'

'My father has been unwell, that is enough reason to have refrained from announcements and celebrations. This photo, of the night I made a commitment to you, is enough testimony of our love.'

It *was* love.

She had never truly thought she would know it.

Not fully.

An unrequited version perhaps, if she remained with Alim. Or a diluted version if she attempted to move on and meet someone else.

Yet the man she loved had changed his world for a chance for them. And he told her now why he had.

'Gabi, I never considered love important. I grew up in a loveless, albeit privileged home. I saw first-hand the pain love caused for my father and Fleur…'

He thought back to when love had first started to arrive in his heart.

'When I came to buy the Grande Lucia you were setting up for a wedding. It was the first time I saw you.'

Gabi thought back.

'No, the first time we saw each other was the day after a wedding. You had come back for a second viewing of the hotel…'

'No.'

And Gabi realised then that he had memories of her that she did not know, that the days she had felt so invisible had been days when she had, in fact, been noticed.

'Marry me?' he said, and she nodded.

'Oh, yes.'

'There is only one problem.'

And here it came, Gabi thought, the downside, for she could not remain on this cloud for ever. She braced herself for impact.

'It has to be now.'

Gabi frowned. 'Now?'

'We're already late for our own wedding.'

'You mean *now*!'

'The Sultan of Sultans has chosen. I was lucky to buy us even a few days. I have my family gathered, and I went and spoke with your mother; she has given her blessing if you say yes.'

'When did you speak with my mother?'

'That is why I was late to meet Lucia.'

Gabi was lying in bed on her wedding day when surely there was so much to be done.

'Alim…' She sat up. 'I haven't…'

There was panic, because she was a wedding planner after all and this wedding was her very own.

'There is nothing for you to do. I know you would have dreamed of this day and that it might not be quite what you had planned…'

'No.' Gabi shook her head. 'I never thought of my own.'

'There will be a bigger celebration in Zethlehan but for today everything is under control.'

Except the bride!

For instead of answering her million questions Alim got dressed and then, having read her note with a smile, he left.

Gabi sat in the unmade bed, unsure what she was supposed to do, so she called her mum.

'I am so happy for you,' Carmel said. 'It meant everything that he came and spoke with me…'

'You'll be there?'

'Of course,' her mother said. 'I'm at the hotel now with Lucia and we're both being very spoiled. I shall see you at the wedding.'

It seemed everyone knew what was happening except Gabi and just when she was starting to think she must have misunderstood the bedside phone rang.

'Gabi…'

Gabi rolled her eyes at the familiar voice.

'I can't work today,' Gabi started, but then realised that Bernadetta wasn't calling her to ask her to work.

'If you'd like to put on a robe, the bridal suite is ready for you.'

'For me?'

'Gabi, I haven't been avoiding your calls. Well perhaps a bit, but I've been very busy arranging a royal wedding in Rome, with only five days' notice. Thank goodness I'm good at my job!'

Gabi had always resented that Alim seemed one step ahead of her.

She didn't today.

Yes, Bernadetta was a right royal pain, but she was the best in the business.

Gabi almost felt sorry for Bernadetta for the panic she must have had to arrange such a rapid wedding.

Almost!

CHAPTER SEVENTEEN

GABI KNOCKED ON the door of the Grande Lucia's bridal suite.

She knew it very well, but usually she was carrying flowers or had her arms piled high with a wedding dress.

Today she had nothing, not even her purse, for in the confusion she had left it all behind.

The door to the suite opened and there stood Bernadetta. Gabi's nerves didn't quite disappear but they faded as, even from a distance, Alim made her smile.

Gone was the black suit.

Bernadetta looked amazing in a willow-green and pale pink check suit—and, yes, Alim really had thought of it all.

'You have nothing to worry about,' Bernadetta said as Gabi stepped in. 'I've been working closely with Alim and Violetta and everything is under control. But first I have something for you from me.'

Bernadetta handed her a box, and when Gabi opened it she saw that they were business cards.

They were the palest blush-pink with a trail of willow-green ivy and the lettering was in gold.

Matrimoni Internazionali di Gabriella.

'No.' Gabi went to put the card back in its box; this wasn't how she wanted it to be. 'I don't want Alim buying me a career.'

'Gabi,' Bernadetta said, 'I had a long think after our discussion. Of course I was furious at the suggestion, but when I had calmed down I thought about it properly. It is too much for one person. I was going to offer you a junior partnership. I don't want to lose you and when Alim called and asked if I would arrange the wedding, well, I knew I was about to so I had to think on my feet. I came up with this. Gabi, you're going to be overseas a lot and I hope back here often…'

Gabi nodded.

'We can work all the details out, but together we can make a success of it.'

And her heart started to soar because Bernadetta was right—married to a sultan, a career would be hard without back-up, but in a partnership, well, perhaps it could work for them both.

And there was something else too.

'It's been a tough few years in the industry,' Bernadetta said, 'but things have been starting to turn around and it's in no small part thanks to you.'

Oh, it wasn't just the suit, but Bernadetta looked lighter, younger and more relaxed. Maybe this partnership would take some of the pressure from her too.

But as exciting as the future was, there was really only one partnership on Gabi's mind today.

The door opened to hair and make-up artists and while they set up Gabi went and had a bath.

It was so wonderful to relax, knowing that Lucia was being taken care of and that soon she and Alim would be married. That on the day he met his daughter for the first time, a family they became for real.

After the bath she unwrapped some packages to discover the underwear was a soft white gauze and just what Gabi would have chosen.

It was subtle but terribly sexy and she was glad to hide it under a robe when she stepped out.

Gabi's hair was curled and pinned up, leaving a few long coils to fall, and then the make-up artist got to work under instruction from Bernadetta as Gabi closed her eyes.

'Not too much!' Gabi warned, because she wasn't big on make-up and it felt as if it was being piled on.

'Perfetto,' Bernadetta said, and Gabi opened her eyes. But sheets had been put over the many mirrors. 'I want you to see the full effect all at once.'

'What if I don't like it?'

'Then we keep the groom waiting until you do.' Bernadetta shrugged. 'But I know you are going to love it.'

The door opened again and this time it was Rosa, and Gabi found that she was nervous as the dress was unveiled.

There was no need to be.

Rosa had worked magic indeed.

It was a pale ivory and reminded her of the robe she had worn in the desert.

As Bernadetta did up the row of tiny buttons at the back, Gabi found she was shaking. It was starting to sink in that she would soon be Alim's wife.

The shoes chosen for her had just a little heel and then the door opened and it was Angela with the flowers.

Gabi had to fight not to cry when she saw them.

A bunch of sweet peas and all paper white.

'I wanted to add some gardenias but Alim was adamant. Do you know,' Angela said as she looked at the exquisite trail of blooms, 'I think this is the best I have ever made.'

Each bloom was so delicate and fragrant and perfect that there was nothing—not a single wisp of anything—that Gabi would add to them.

And then Bernadetta took the sheet from the full-length mirror and Gabi, who had never dared to even imagine herself as one, looked back at the bride.

'Oh, Gabi,' Bernadetta said.

And Gabi just stared. The dress hung beautifully and did nothing to play down her curves; her eyes were smoky and her lipstick pale and, no, she could not have chosen better.

'Are you ready?' Bernadetta asked.

'So ready—I would run if I could.'

'You would fall,' Bernadetta said. 'And I don't have a spare dress for you to change into.'

It was a smiling bride who turned heads as she walked through the foyer of the Grande Lucia and stood outside the double doors of the ballroom.

And then nerves caught up with her.

'Just walk straight ahead,' Bernadetta told her. 'Gabi, all you have to do is enjoy every moment.'

She stepped in and there in that ballroom was everyone she loved, and for a moment she looked and tried to take it all in.

Her mother looked gorgeous and was holding Lucia, who wore a little mink-coloured dress and showed one little dark curl.

And when she got over her joy, and when they had made love as man and wife, there would be questions—so many of them.

Fleur was there and she stood next to James and Mona and, a couple of rows ahead, sat a very handsome, exotic-looking middle-aged man.

Oh, there were secrets in every family and mysteries too, but there was now no shame in the al-Lehans.

Alim did not want to know if this man was the reason his mother knew love.

Gabi, curious by nature, would be certain to find out!

Yes, Violetta had her work cut out with this family and, Gabi suspected, the adjoining rooms at the Grande Lucia would be creaking tonight.

Bastiano was there, and Sophie was too.

It dawned on Gabi then the reason she had been around so much these past days, she had been keeping an eye on the bride while so many plans were underway.

'You knew!' she mouthed to her dear friend as she walked past, and Sophie laughed.

The only person missing was the groom.

And then nerves caught up.

There was his errant sister and Alim's brother, Kaleb, and beside them was the queen, but most intimidating of all was the Sultan of Sultans, who, as Gabi nervously approached, stepped forward.

He spoke first in Arabic, which Gabi did not understand, but then he spoke again.

'The Sultan of Sultans has chosen.'

Gabi saw Alim then.

He wore a robe of silver, but it was the love for her in his eyes that brought tears to hers.

He took her hands and she felt the warmth of his fingers as they caressed hers; his voice was low and for Gabi's ears only.

'He chose wisely.'

Gabi always felt that she shone under Alim's gaze, and this moment was no exception.

They knelt on the gorgeous floor and were blessed, and then they rose as man and wife.

'Are you happy?' he asked.

'So happy,' Gabi said, and then she smiled. 'What if I'd said no?'

'Are you cross now at my assumption that you would agree to marry me?'

'No.'

For it told her of his certainty in them.

And as he moved in to kiss his bride Alim told her a truth.

'This is love,' he whispered, 'and it's ours for ever.'

* * * * *

Don't forget to read the first part of
Carol Marinelli's
BILLIONAIRES AND ONE-NIGHT HEIRS
miniseries

THE INNOCENT'S SECRET BABY
Available now!

And look out for the third and final instalment—
coming soon!

#3533 HER SINFUL SECRET
The Disgraced Copelands
by Jane Porter

Logan finds herself at Rowan Argyros's mercy when he discovers their secret daughter, but she cannot forget how he took her virginity and heartlessly rejected her. Rowan longs to claim her—but will her craving for his touch persuade her into marriage?

#3534 THE PRINCE'S NINE-MONTH SCANDAL
Scandalous Royal Brides
by Caitlin Crews

When personal assistant Natalie Monette discovers her secret identical twin, Princess Valentina, they decide to swap lives. Suddenly, her "fiancé" Crown Prince Rodolfo finds himself feeling a desire he cannot understand...until he discovers who's carrying the consequence of their passion!

#3535 THE DRAKON BABY BARGAIN
The Drakon Royals
by Tara Pammi

When Princess Eleni is offered a convenient marriage by Drakon's biggest investor, Gabriel Marquez, she strikes her own deal—she'll get a child of her own, he'll get a mother for his daughter. Except neither had predicted the fire that rages between them...

#3536 THE GREEK'S PLEASURABLE REVENGE
Secret Heirs of Billionaires
by Andie Brock

The last person Calista wants to see is Lukas Kalanos, who stole her innocence and left her with much more than a broken heart. On discovering her child is theirs, Lukas's pleasurable plans of revenge become a hunger to make her his!

Get 2 Free Books,
Plus 2 Free Gifts—
just for trying the
Reader Service!

YES! Please send me 2 FREE Harlequin Presents® novels and my 2 FREE gifts (gifts are worth about $10 retail). After receiving them, if I don't wish to receive any more books, I can return the shipping statement marked "cancel." If I don't cancel, I will receive 6 brand-new novels every month and be billed just $4.55 each for the regular-print edition or $5.55 each for the larger-print edition in the U.S., or $5.49 each for the regular-print edition or $5.99 each for the larger-print edition in Canada. That's a saving of at least 11% off the cover price! It's quite a bargain! Shipping and handling is just 50¢ per book in the U.S. and 75¢ per book in Canada.* I understand that accepting the 2 free books and gifts places me under no obligation to buy anything. I can always return a shipment and cancel at any time. Even if I never buy another book, the 2 free books and gifts are mine to keep forever.

Please check one: ☐ Harlequin Presents® Regular-Print   ☐ Harlequin Presents® Larger-Print
                          (106/306 HDN GLP6)   (176/376 HDN GLP7)

Name _____ (PLEASE PRINT) _____

Address _____ Apt. # _____

City _____ State/Prov. _____ Zip/Postal Code _____

Signature (if under 18, a parent or guardian must sign)

Mail to the **Reader Service:**
IN U.S.A.: P.O. Box 1867, Buffalo, NY 14240-1867
IN CANADA: P.O. Box 611, Fort Erie, Ontario L2A 9Z9

**Want to try two free books from another series? Call 1-800-873-8635 or
visit www.ReaderService.com.**

* Terms and prices subject to change without notice. Prices do not include applicable taxes. Sales tax applicable in N.Y. Canadian residents will be charged applicable taxes. Offer not valid in Quebec. This offer is limited to one order per household. Books received may not be as shown. Not valid for current subscribers to Harlequin Presents books. All orders subject to credit approval. Credit or debit balances in a customer's account(s) may be offset by any other outstanding balance owed by or to the customer. Please allow 4 to 6 weeks for delivery. Offer available while quantities last.

Your Privacy—The Reader Service is committed to protecting your privacy. Our Privacy Policy is available online at www.ReaderService.com or upon request from the Reader Service.

We make a portion of our mailing list available to reputable third parties that offer products we believe may interest you. If you prefer that we not exchange your name with third parties, or if you wish to clarify or modify your communication preferences, please visit us at www.ReaderService.com/consumerschoice or write to us at Reader Service Preference Service, P.O. Box 9062, Buffalo, NY 14240-9062. Include your complete name and address.

HP17R

SPECIAL EXCERPT FROM

H HARLEQUIN

Presents.

*Ruthless Prince Adam Katsaros offers Belle a deal—
he'll release her father if she becomes his mistress!
Adam's gaze awakens a heated desire in Belle. Her
innocent beauty might redeem his royal reputation—but
can she tame the beast inside…?*

*Read on for a sneak preview of
THE PRINCE'S CAPTIVE VIRGIN,
the first part of Maisey Yates's
ONCE UPON A SEDUCTION… trilogy.*

"You really are kind of a beast," Belle said, standing up.
Adam caught her wrist, stopped her from leaving.

"And what bothers you most about that? The fact that
you would like to reform me, that you would like for your
time here to mean something and you are beginning to
see that it won't? Or is it the fact that you don't want to
reform me at all, and that you rather like me this way? Or
at least, your body likes me this way."

"Bodies make stupid decisions all the time. My father
wanted my mother, and she was a terrible, unloving person
who didn't even want her own daughter. So, forgive me if
I find this argument rather uncompelling. It doesn't make
you a good person, just because I enjoy kissing you. And
it doesn't make this something worth exploring."

She broke free of him and began to walk away, striding
down the hall, back toward her room. He pushed away
from the table, letting his chair fall to the floor, not caring
enough to right it as he followed after Belle.

He caught up to her, pivoting so that he was in front of her. She took a step backward, then to the side, butting up against the wall. Then he caged her between his arms, staring down at her. Her blue eyes were glittering, her breasts rising and falling rapidly with each breath.

"This is the only thing worth exploring. Not what could be, but what you have. The fire that burns between you and another person. For all you know, in the days since you've been here the entire world has fallen away. And if we were all that was left…would you not regret missing out on the chance to see how hot we could burn?"

She shook her head. "But the world hasn't fallen away," she said, her trembling lips pale now, a complete contrast to the rich color they had been only moments ago. "It's still there. And whatever happens in here will have consequences out there. I will help you, Adam, but I'm not going to give you my body. I'm not going to destroy that life that I have out there to play games with you in here. You're a stranger to me, and you're going to remain a stranger to me. I can pretend. I can give you whatever you need when it comes to making a statement for your country. But beyond that? I can't."

Then she turned and walked away, and this time, he let her go.

Don't miss
THE PRINCE'S CAPTIVE VIRGIN
available June 2017 wherever
Harlequin Presents® books and ebooks are sold.

www.Harlequin.com

HARLEQUIN
Presents®

Next month, look out for *The Prince's Nine-Month Scandal*
by Caitlin Crews, the first part of her sinfully exciting new
duet, Scandalous Royal Brides!

Natalie and Valentina cannot believe their eyes…they're the very
image of one another, so similar they could be identical twins. They
agree to swap identities for six weeks—but what will happen when
the alpha heroes closest to them uncover the outrageous truth?

Natalie Monette's life is transformed by meeting Valentina—but
Valentina is unhappily engaged to the supremely arrogant Crown
Prince Rodolfo. Natalie's plan is to put arrogant Rodolfo in his
place…until she's enticed by the heat between them!

Prince Rodolfo can't understand why, having *never* felt any desire
for his betrothed, he now can't keep his hands off this captivating
woman. But scandal abounds when he discovers who he's shared
such passion with…and that she's carrying his heir!

Don't miss

The Prince's Nine-Month Scandal

Available June 2017

And discover Princess Valentina and Achilles Casilieris's story

The Billionaire's Secret Princess

Available July 2017

Stay Connected:

www.Harlequin.com

f /HarlequinBooks

🐦 @HarlequinBooks

P /HarlequinBooks

HP06068